Opposites Attract

Heartlines

Books by Pam Lyons

A Boy Called Simon
He Was Bad
It Could Never Be
Latchkey Girl
Danny's Girl
Odd Girl Out
Ms Perfect

Books by Anita Eires

Tug Of Love
Summer Awakening
Spanish Exchange
Star Dreamer
Californian Summer
If Only . . .
Teacher's Pet
Working Girl

Books by Mary Hooper

Love Emma XXX
Follow That Dream
My Cousin Angie
Happy Ever After
Opposites Attract

Books by Barbara Jacobs

Two Times Two

Books by Jane Pitt

Loretta Rose

Autumn Always Comes
Stony Limits
Rainbows For Sale

Books by Ann de Gale

Island Encounter
Hands Off

Books by Anthea Cohen

Dangerous Love

Books by David S. Williams

Give Me Back My Pride
Forgive and Forget

Books by Jill Young

Change Of Heart

Books by Ann Ruffell

Friends For Keeps
Secret Passion

Books by Lorna Read

Images
The Name Is 'Zero'

Books by Jane Butterworth

Spotlight On Sam

Heartlines

Mary Hooper

Opposites Attract

A Pan Original

First published 1986 by Pan Books Ltd,
Cavaye Place, London SW10 9PG

9 8 7 6 5 4 3 2 1

© Mary Hooper 1986

ISBN 0 330 29181 5

Made and printed in Great Britain by
Hunt Barnard Printing Ltd, Aylesbury, Bucks.

Chapter One

'Mandy!' Mum called up the stairs. Instead of replying, I crawled a bit deeper into the cupboard.

'Amanda!' She was getting cross but I didn't care. I wanted to be on my own, just for ten minutes. Let one of the others go down the shops for her.

'Vicky! See if you can find Mandy for me, will you?' she said then, and there was a bang as Vicky flung open the door of our bedroom in her usual careless way and it crashed against the wall. The wallpaper had worn just at that point, revealing a small patch of crumbling plaster, indicating how often she did it.

'She's not here!' she called down, and although I couldn't hear Mum tutting, I knew she was.

'Then you and Vanessa will have to go,' Mum said.

'Oh, Mummy,' I heard Vicky whine. 'We were just going out to play and . . .'

The whining receded downstairs and I relaxed – with some difficulty in such a confined space. All morning it had been hectic: records and radio blaring out, arguments, kids coming and going, orders to do things, beds being changed under you – a girl just couldn't *think*.

I switched on my torch. I was in a long, low cupboard with a sloping roof in the corner of the bedroom I shared with the twins. In front of me was a great jumbled pile of plastic toys, most of them broken, and in front of those stood a huge dolls' house made by one of our uncles and containing a doll family and about as much furniture as Buckingham Palace. It was out of favour just then, though, and sat jammed, unlooked-at and unloved, halfway down the cupboard.

I'd earlier discovered that over behind the dolls' house there's a space a couple of metres long and about a metre high and wide that no one knows about. I've made it my own secret space, my special place. I've got an old rug, a torch and a pile of books in there. It might not sound much to someone who's got a bedroom to themselves – it probably sounds altogether batty, come to think of it, squatting in a cupboard – but to me it's bliss.

It's the only place I can be on my own, you see. The only place in the whole house where no one can get to me. It's there I go when I want to be private, especially when I want to sit and think thoughts about Leo Mann. Leo Mann . . . I think it's a fantastic name, like a pop star's or something, but Leo's just a boy at school.

Actually, I don't mean *just* a boy at school, Leo's a lot more to me than that. He's tall and fair with blond streaks in his hair and he always looks slightly tanned, even in winter. He's also got the most incredible sea-green eyes that are sometimes clear and sometimes misty-looking. I spend a lot of time in the cupboard writing him letters that never get sent and drawing hearts with our initials in them – daft things like that. Mostly I just think about him, though.

When you've got a big family like mine, getting away to think about things is practically impossible. I'm the middle one of five, you see. First there's Rachel, she's twenty, then Tim – eighteen and the only boy. I come next at sixteen, and you would have thought three children enough for anyone, wouldn't you? But no, Mum had to go on and have twins six years later: Vicky and Vanessa. I wouldn't object to *them* so much if Mum didn't make so much fuss of them. But twins, of course, are regarded as something special. When they were little, Mum used to dress them alike – usually something pink and frilly – and push them out in their double pushchair to admiring gasps from old ladies. I can remember it well, hanging on the arm of the pushchair and being ignored while everyone cooed over Vanessa and Vicky and said what pretty children they were and had Mum ever thought of putting them in advertisements because they were so *gorgeous*, really they were.

It's not much better now. I'm not exactly jealous of them, but I can't help resenting them a bit. I suppose, if I'm honest, I could resent all my family for something. You see, Rachel's special because she's the oldest, Tim's special because he's the only boy, Vicky and Vanessa are special because they're twins. I'm just an also-ran, no one special at all.

Some day I will be, though, and I can't *wait*. I'm going to have my own little flat – none of that four-girls-sharing rubbish for me, I've had enough of sharing – a good job, and be someone special in my own right.

Fifteen minutes after I'd crawled into the cupboard, I heard the twins come back from shopping. I switched off the torch and clambered out into the room; I didn't want them to come up with me still in there or I could be stuck for ages. By the time they appeared I was lying on my bed, pretending to read.

'Where have you been?' Vicky said in astonishment. 'I came up here looking for you just now.'

'You couldn't have looked very well, then,' I said.

'*We* had to go to the shops for Mummy instead of you,' Vanessa put in.

'I've been up here all the time, I promise.'

'Not on your bed, I looked!'

I gave a shrug. 'I might have been sitting on the floor on the other side.'

Vicky clearly didn't believe me. 'But Mummy was calling. You must have heard her.'

'*Was* she?'

'Were you hiding in here?' Vanessa asked.

'How could I have been? Where is there to hide in here?'

They looked at each other, eyes narrowed suspiciously. They are identical all right; with outsiders you always get that boring: 'And which twin are *you*?' routine. Both have the same smooth, round faces with little snub noses and the gingery-fair hair that we've all got. They are both growing their fringes out so at any given time one of them will bend over, run her fingers through her fringe to flick it backwards out of her eyes, then bob up again. When they do it they look like those toy chickens drinking out of a glass of water – and it really gets on my nerves.

'It's very funny, anyway,' Vanessa said, frowning.

Vicky bent over, flicked and bounced up again, then went and jumped on her bed. They've got bunk beds on the opposite wall to mine and Vicky, on the bottom one, has made hers into a little camp. She's got an old sheet pulled all the way down from Vanessa's bed and has papered her section of wall with loads of pictures of kittens — she's mad on them. There are pictures stuck on the underside of Vanessa's mattress, too, poked between the springs, so that even when she's lying down and looking straight up she can see kittens.

'What are you reading?' Vanessa asked. She put out her hand to take my book but I jerked it away.

'Nothing to do with you.'

'One of those soppy love books, I bet,' she said. 'Slobber, slobber, slurp, slurp . . .'

Vicky giggled shrilly. 'Is it rude? Kirstie brought a book into school yesterday where a boy touched a girl's bosom.' They both shrieked with laughter.

'Oh, honestly,' I said with as much dignity as I could.

'Has that book got bosoms in it?'

'Go on, let's see!' Vanessa made a grab for the book and I shoved her so that she staggered away.

'I'll tell Mummy! You really hurt me!'

'Go away, you *silly* little girl,' I said witheringly, and she jumped into Vicky' camp and I could hear them giggling together in there.

I rolled over on my bed so I was facing away from them and tried to read. It was no good though, because when they're in the same room I can't read or think or do homework; all I can do is feel irritated.

My greatest wish is that Rachel will leave home so

that I can have her bedroom. She'll never get married, though; no one will have her because she's too frumpy and bad-tempered. There's always the hope that Tim will go off to college or decide to share a flat with someone – but I can't see him leaving here because he's got it so jammy: Mum fetches and carries for him and would have the rest of us doing the same if we'd stand for it. He doesn't have to lift a *finger* round the house.

No, the only way I'm going to get any privacy, any breathing space, is if I go. And just as soon as I've got a job and can support myself I'll be out like a shot.

'Where *is* everyone?' I heard Mum call from downstairs. 'Lunch is ready!'

The twins dived from underneath the sheet overhang and went into forward rolls along the carpet as if they were bursting into a room to avoid gunfire; they'd obviously been watching too many cops-and-robbers films on television. Vicky managed hers all right but Vanessa went clumsily sideways and her leg hit the cupboard – she's not as agile as Vicky. I went downstairs and they followed me, still giggling and talking about bosoms, obviously in one of their silly moods.

As it was Saturday, Mum had prepared some homemade soup. She always refuses to cook 'properly' on a Saturday so we have soup at lunchtime and then one of us usually goes out to fetch fish and chips for supper.

The table was laid in the kitchen. Well, I say 'laid' but it just had salt and pepper on it; Mum is never properly organized.

'Get the spoons out, someone! Mandy, get the big

soup bowls down!' Mum said breathlessly. She's always in a last-minute rush, probably because she tries to do six things at once.

As Mum ladled out the soup, Dad came in from the garden, Rachel appeared from upstairs and Tim came in from the front where he'd been repairing a motor-bike.

I looked round: chaos! Mum had obviously been distracted while preparing the vegetables because there was a big pile of peelings sitting on the chopping board and the whole place looked like one of those insurance advertisements where the burglars have been in and wrecked everything. As well as the vegetable peelings on the worktop there was an iron, three saucepans, three pints of milk, an empty tea packet, various knives – Dad always says Mum uses every knife and fork in the place when she's cooking anything – a sieve, a blender bearing traces of soup all over it, the plastic bin the potatoes are kept in, and a pair of slippers; *a pair of slippers*! In other words, it was a real mess. Mum is so slap-dash, it drives me wild.

I sighed as I sat down but no one heard me, they were all too busy talking.

'Eat up, dear,' Mum said. She's not happy unless everyone's jaws are going up and down.

'How's the school magazine?' Tim asked, and I looked at him gratefully. He was the only one who'd remembered. Last term a few of us had got together and decided it would be fun to bring out a school magazine; nothing serious or heavy, just school news and pop, quizzes and book reviews – that sort of thing, and we'd just about started getting our ideas into shape.

'Fine,' I said, 'but hardly off the ground yet. We're still discussing content at the moment.'

'Who're you doing it with? Not Sammy?'

I rolled my eyes. My friend Sammy is my best friend but she's more than a bit fluffy. She hadn't been the slightest bit interested when I'd told her about the plans for the magazine – and then she'd decided not to stay on at school anyway.

'Thought not,' Tim said. 'All she'd be good for was writing about how to turn your eyelids purple.'

'She's not that bad,' I said. 'Anyway, she's not at school now, is she? No, I'm co-editing it with one of the boys.'

'Anyone I know?'

'I don't think so.' Had my voice gone squeaky? 'It's Leo,' I said casually. 'Leo Mann.' I waited for everyone to go quiet and the twins to look at me and squeal: 'Is he your boyfriend?' like they did whenever they saw me within two hundred metres of a boy, but they didn't on this occasion. 'Leo Mann,' I said again. It was nice saying his name out loud, bringing it into the conversation.

'What's he contributing, then?'

'Oh, he's going to concentrate on the technical stuff, write articles about computers and review software and all that.'

'Yeah?' Tim held up his bowl for more soup; Mum ran to get it.

'He's really clever,' I said. 'He knows more than the teachers about computers. He can explain things, too – he doesn't get too technical so you can't understand what he's going on about.' He's also got these sea-green eyes and . . .

But Tim had stopped being interested in Leo and was waiting for someone to give him more bread. 'If you need any illustrations done,' he said when he remembered me again, 'Jonno said he wouldn't mind doing them for you.'

'Great,' I said. Tim's friend Jonathan goes to art college and is training to be a graphic designer. 'I don't know what we'll need yet, though.'

Tim shrugged. 'Just let him know.'

I finished my soup and listened with half an ear to Mum and Rachel discussing the whereabouts of the latter's best blouse.

'You know the one, it's got tucks down the front,' she said. 'I specially asked if it could be ready for tonight.'

'Well, I don't know I'm sure,' Mum said. 'I can't remember ironing it. Have you checked the airing cupboard.'

'I've checked everywhere,' Rachel said crossly. 'If I can't find it I don't know what I'll do.'

'Don't be silly, dear, you've got plenty of other blouses.'

'Not like this one.' Rachel glanced suspiciously round the table, eyes narrowed and looking remarkably like the twins had done earlier. She's got the same pale complexion and silly nose as they have, and the same colour hair, of course, but hers is as curly as theirs is straight so it always looks as if she's got a frumpy, tight perm. 'I hope no one's borrowed it,' she said.

'Who would?' Mum asked. 'It's too big for the twins and I can't see Tim in it.'

'What about Mandy . . .'

I shook my head violently. 'Catch me in that! The nylon one with bits down the front? It's an old woman's blouse!'

'The trouble with you is you don't know class when you see it,' Rachel snapped. 'Just because you go to those cheap and nasty little fashion shops . . .'

'Well, I haven't had your blouse,' I said indignantly. Honestly, I get picked on for everything. 'I wouldn't use it for a polishing rag!'

'Now, now,' Mum began, and Dad banged on the table.

'I'm only here for two days a week,' he said, 'so how is it that whenever I'm home there's a quarrel?'

'They're *always* bickering, dear,' Mum said mildly. 'If you were here all the time you'd get used to it, like I have.'

Dad scraped his chair back and stood up. 'God help me when I retire, then,' he said. 'I'm going out in the garden for some peace.'

He went. Mum organized the washing up and then the phone rang. It was Sammy, for me.

'Hi, want to come round?' she said.

'If you like. I've got nothing better to do.'

'Well, thanks very much!' she said.

I laughed. 'You know what I mean.'

I heard her yawning. 'It's really boring here. Everyone's gone out and there's nothing to do.'

I pictured her sprawled on her stairs, surrounded by *acres* of lovely space and silence. She's an only child and both her parents work full time.

'I'll come as soon as I can,' I said. 'I want to look at some school magazine stuff first.'

'Don't be long, then.'

'Can't you do something while you wait for me? Read a book!'

'Can't get into anything,' she moaned. 'Hurry up.'

I put the phone down. Sammy never can 'get into' books, as she puts it. She can't get into much else either – apart from make-up and clothes, that is. She likes boys, too, of course. Boys in general and one called Graham Price in particular.

'If you're going upstairs, take something from the pile!' Mum called from the kitchen, so though I was halfway up I went down again and retrieved the pile of things placed on the bottom stair; anything to make the house look a bit more presentable. There's always a pile of stuff waiting to go up, and at the top a similar pile waiting to come down, and as each item disappears to its rightful home another magically appears to take its place. Today there were: two bath towels and swimming costumes, a packet of loo rolls, a tube of toothpaste, three new pairs of underpants still in their wrapping, a pot plant belonging to the bathroom, a screwdriver, a light bulb and, right at the bottom and folded neatly, Rachel's argued-about blouse.

'Your blouse is here, Rachel, on the stairs!' I shouted.

She came out of the kitchen and looked at me accusingly. 'How did it get there?'

'How would I know?'

She shook it out. 'It's all creased,' she said crossly. 'It'll have to be ironed again.'

'But at least I've found it for you,' I said pointedly. 'You won't have to go out in your bra.'

She gave me a grudging sort of smile. 'Yes. Thanks, Mandy.'

I took the rest of the pile upstairs and dumped it all in the bathroom. Let someone else sort it out.

I went into my bedroom and scrabbled under the bed for my school bag. Leo had been working on our school magazine stuff for two days and had left it on my locker last thing the afternoon before, and I hadn't yet had time to look at his ideas for a cover. I was supposed to come up with a few points so we could discuss them in our free period on Monday.

I pulled out the green file containing all the material. Everything was neatly indexed and clipped together – Mum says she can never understand where I get my tidy nature from, that I must be a throw-back to *her* mother – and there was a transparent envelope marked 'cover ideas'.

I pulled out a few black and white sketches and an envelope came with them; an envelope with 'Mandy Rossiter' written on it in Leo's clear, neat handwriting. A letter for me from Leo – I'd had the file for a whole day and I hadn't thought to look before!

Dear Mandy [it said],
I won't have a chance to see you (I've got running practice after school) but I've enclosed the cover ideas. They aren't all that brilliant.

We'll have to meet out of school to go over everything, I think, and decide who else needs to be brought in to help. Perhaps you could come round one evening, or I could come to your house?

I stopped reading, my hand shook. A date! It was practically a date! I went back to the letter.

I'm enjoying doing it all, hope you are. I think we make a good team!
Love, Leo.

Love, Leo . . . I traced the words with my fingertips. He'd actually written those, to me. Love, Leo . . . he'd sent me his love and wanted to see me . . . A smile slid across my face to be replaced a moment later by a look of panic. How on earth could I ask him here, to this dump? How could we sit here amid the chaos and mess and noise? How could we talk with the twins nearby squealing, giggling and asking – oh God! – if he'd seen my bosoms?

I couldn't bring him here; I'd die. No, we'd have to go to his house. I pictured it: a calm oasis, dim lights, soft music. His mother (his father was dead) conveniently out for the evening so there would be just the two of us discussing things in low, intimate terms with lots of looking into each other's eyes . . .

Vicky burst into the room and the door banged against the wall. A few flakes of plaster fell on the carpet.

She looked at me and her eyes immediately fell on the letter.

'Is that from a boy?' she demanded. She doesn't miss a trick, that one.

Vanessa bounded in, bounced down and flicked her fringe out of her eyes and bounced up again. I put my letter away.

'It is from a boy, isn't it?' Vicky said. 'What's it say?'

'Nothing to do with little girls like you,' I said loftily.

'I'll tell Mum. I'll tell everyone.'

'Tell who you like,' I said.

'We'll get it and read it if you don't tell us,' Vanessa said, joining in. 'We'll read it to *everyone*.'

'You'll have to find it first, won't you?'

I picked up the file, tucked it under my arm and went out of the door. I was aware of the smile on my face: I'd got a letter from Leo and I felt as if I might remain smiling for the rest of my life.

At the bottom of the stairs was a new pile waiting to be transported. I ignored it. In the kitchen I could hear Mum doing her best to stop a quarrel between Rachel and Tim.

'I'm going to Sammy's!' I shouted to whoever was listening. 'I'm getting away from this madhouse!'

Chapter Two

I couldn't help looking over my shoulder all the way to Sammy's house. I get this feeling sometimes about the twins – that they're following me about; spying on me. Maybe I've been watching too many cops and robbers as well – but I wouldn't put it past them, really I wouldn't.

I had quite a walk before I got off our estate. It's a council one, or it *was* a council one; most of the people living in the houses have bought them now, including Mum and Dad.

Sammy's house is across the railway line: the right side of the tracks, you might say, and Leo lives this side of town, too. Leo . . . I hugged the magazine file a bit closer to myself as if I was cuddling him instead of just his letter.

Funny, I hadn't really known Leo at all until a few months ago. I failed my maths 'O' level, you see, failed it miserably, so Mum insisted that I stay on and get a place in the school's sixth form in order to re-take it. I wasn't at all keen, especially as Sammy had got herself a job, but Mum said it was important, that I wouldn't get anywhere without my maths 'O' level, so that was that.

I'd discovered, luckily, that I liked the Sixth a lot better than normal school. Firstly, we had no proper uniform – just our own choice of navy skirt and white top – and secondly, thirdly and fourthly, Leo was in it. Leo's old school had had no Sixth so he'd had to transfer to ours to take his 'A' levels. He wanted to be a journalist so the magazine idea had been his mostly, but as soon as he mentioned it I found I was really keen, too. Mind you, I wasn't sure if I'd have been half so enthusiastic about it if it had been spotty Dave Hawkins or gormless Mick Hattersly who'd come up with the idea.

Walking to Sammy's took about ten minutes. I had to cross through Hurst Green where (rumour had it) Leo lived, and I glanced in the windows as I walked by, wondering if I might see him.

No luck, though – and the houses were set so far back from the road, with hedges and trees in front (it was *that* sort of estate), that I didn't get much of a view anyway.

Sammy was watching from her bedroom window for me. She waved wildly and ran to open the door.

'Ta-ra!' she said, and moved her head from side to side so that I could get the benefit of her new hairdo. 'What d'you think, then? Wild, eh?'

I stared at her. It was wild all right – standing away from her head almost horizontally in layers of blonde frizz. She was always doing something to herself; I'd never known a girl change her hairstyle, make-up and clothes as frequently as she did. 'How did you do it?'

'Well,' she said, 'first I did it in little plaits all over – it took *ages* – then I sprayed it with a mixture of water and setting gel, then I dried it thoroughly and *then* I took it all out and back-combed it. D'you like it?'

I hesitated and then nodded. I did like it – but only someone like Sammy could get away with it. 'It's great,' I said. 'You look like one of Bananarama.'

'Good,' she said, 'that's just who I wanted to look like.' She went towards the stairs. 'Come up, I'm just about dying of boredom. It's so quiet now that Mum's working on Saturdays.'

'Where's your Dad, then?'

She waved her hand dismissively. 'Gone to play squash or something.'

'Couldn't you have gone with him?'

She looked at me as if I was mad. 'Run round a little glass box after a ball? Catch me doing that.'

I shrugged. 'It would have been something to do.'

She pushed open the door to her bedroom. Her own, wonderfully twin-less bedroom.

'I've got this great new beauty magazine with some fantastic ideas for eyes. Really zany!'

I followed her in. Her bedroom didn't have quite the same air of well-kept calm as the rest of the house because every available inch seemed to be covered with different types of make-up, especially eye make-up. Sammy had once been told by a boy that she had 'bloody fantastic eyes' and since then she'd played up her eyes for all they were worth. I'd seen them every colour of the rainbow and all the shades in between, with painted-on stars at the corners, with great lightning flashes across, and edged with thick black kohl so she looked like a panda.

'Before we start on all that,' I said, taking the file from under my arm and riffling through it, 'I've got something to show you!' I pulled the letter out and waved it. 'A letter from Leo!'

21

She looked amazed and delighted, as I'd known she would. 'A real letter from him, through the post?'

'Not quite that good,' I said. 'It's just to do with the magazine really.'

'Oh,' she said. She took it from me and read it out loud. 'I think we make a great team,' she repeated when she'd finished. '*That* sounds a bit meaningful.'

'That's what I thought.'

'Right! No holds barred on Monday. Make sure he gets the message. Flutter your eyelashes a bit and look suggestively at him across the Sixth form lounge.'

I giggled. 'I *couldn't*!'

''Course you could. Look, like this . . .' She lowered her eyes so that she was peering out of them half-shut and pouted her lips in and out.

'You look like a goldfish!'

She carried on pouting. 'You take it from me, this is the way to get him interested. He'll be eating out of your hand before the week's out.'

'D'you really think so?' I said doubtfully. Leo didn't seem the sort of boy to be led astray by a lot of lash-fluttering and lip-wiggling.

'I'm sure of it. Bet he asks you out next weekend. He'll take you to the pictures in town and you'll have a romantic walk home.'

'In the moonlight,' I put in.

'OK, in the moonlight. And then when you get to your house he'll take you in his arms and . . .'

I groaned loudly. 'Let me finish. When we get to my house he'll take me in his arms and the twins will spring up from behind a hedge and yell: "Our Mandy's snogging with someone!" and then Dad will knock loudly on the window and . . . and Rachel will push past us tutting loudly and we'll end up falling over a bit of Tim's motorbike which he's left on the path.'

Sammy giggled. 'Yeah, it could be like that, knowing your family,' she said, and then she pushed me down in a chair facing the mirror and flung a towel over my shoulders. 'Now be quiet,' she said, 'I'm going to transform you.'

I sat. She worked carefully, her tongue sticking out of the corner of her mouth, making constant referral to the magazine on her worktop. I think she's a frustrated make-up artist or something.

Fifteen minutes later she stood back with another 'Ta-ra!' and I looked at myself in the mirror. I looked *awful*. Sammy had applied purple and pink eyeshadow but instead of making my brown eyes look bigger, like it promised in the magazine, it just sort of closed them up and brought them closer together so that I looked like a ferret. A rather tired ferret.

'Awful!' I said.

She sighed. 'It is really, isn't it? After all that work, too.' She brightened up a bit. 'You do mine now, then.'

'What sort of face d'you want?'

She flicked through the pages of the magazine. 'Do the Night-time Glamour one. With the gold sparkly bits.'

I worked away on her while she told me what sort of a week she'd had at work. She's a trainee receptionist in a big company in town, and the job sounds really boring to me. There are three 'proper' receptionists there and she just sits watching them and supposedly taking everything in. When one of the 'proper' ones goes to lunch then she has a chance to sit in the vacant chair and say: 'Good morning, sir, may I help you?' – that is if one of the other two women doesn't get in first. So far, she's said it exactly six times.

'I don't know how you stand it, really I don't,' I said.

'Oh, it's not so bad. We read. Do our nails. We get a hair-dressing allowance too, because we're always supposed to look well-groomed.'

'Stop talking a sec,' I said, 'I can't get your lips right.' I tissued off what I'd done and tried again, this time with a lip-brush. 'There,' I said, straightening up. 'Finished!'

Sammy fluffed out her hair where I'd flattened it down and looked at her reflection thoughtfully. She had assumed her special mirror look – a coy, shy half-smile.

'Well,' she said, 'it's a bit over-done, isn't it?'

I stared at her shimmering reflection complete with sequins on the cheekbones. 'It *is* called Night-time Glamour . . .' But it *was* a bit overdone, even for Sammy.

'All done up and nowhere to go,' she said.

'Aren't you seeing Graham tonight?'

She nodded. 'Only to go round to his house and watch TV, though.'

'Match of the Day?'

She rolled her eyes. 'Sometimes I don't know why I bother.'

I knew why she bothered, though. She hung onto

Graham because she wanted a boyfriend. Any boyfriend really, just as long as she could say she had one. Graham didn't have a lot going for him as far as I could see, but he was nice-looking and a Casual, which meant he was always smartly dressed, and things like that were important to Sammy.

We cleaned our faces, using one of Sammy's many pots of cleansing cream and tried again. She gave me a 'Daytime Go-anywhere face' and then I did Sammy a 'Zany Fun-face'.

After we'd creamed that little lot off, our faces stung a bit so we just lazed about listening to records for a while.

'It's so nice here. So relaxing,' I said, sighing. 'You can do anything you like and there's no one standing two inches behind you asking why are you doing *that*.'

'It's too quiet, though,' she said. 'Boring.'

I sat up on one elbow and looked at her. 'Go on, be honest — wouldn't you rather be here than at my house?'

'Well . . .' she screwed her nose up. 'It *is* a bit hectic at your place.'

'Exactly!' I said. 'So how could I ever take someone like Leo back there?'

'Maybe he's used to big families.'

'He's got one older brother, away at college,' I said. 'And he's really quiet in himself. He'd probably die of shock if he came within half a mile of my lot.'

'Don't hatch your chickens,' she said, 'he hasn't even asked you out yet. Maybe he won't have to meet the rest of the roaring Rossiters.'

I'm not counting my chickens,' I corrected her, 'it's just that if we're going to get this magazine stuff together we're going to have to see each other out of school anyway. I'll just have to make sure it's not at *my* house.'

'Perhaps you could bribe your family to stay out of the way,' she said, 'or tie them up and put them in a back room or something.'

'Oh, very helpful,' I said.

I left about six o'clock, telling Sammy that I'd ring her in the week and let her know how I'd got on with Leo. Before she'd started going out with Graham we used to see each other on Saturday nights, just to hang around the town square or go for coffee or something, but even that little avenue of pleasure was closed to me now she was seeing him. Still, maybe I'd be going out with Leo on Saturdays before too long.

When I got home and walked into the sitting room the Late, Late Breakfast Show was blaring out from the TV, Barry Manilow was groaning from Rachel's bedroom and Vicky and Vanessa were rolling round and round the floor fighting over a stuffed panda. In the middle of all this sat Dad with his ear to the radio taking down the football results, and Mum calmly reading a magazine.

I looked round in anguish. 'Mum!' I said. 'However can you read? Can't you do something about all the row?'

She looked up. 'It's just everyone doing their own thing,' she said.

'But why can't they do it more quietly?'

26

She smiled. 'I always wanted a big, jolly family and I always say people should feel free to be themselves in their own house. If they can't relax at home where *can* they relax?'

I sighed, but as usual no one heard me because of all the racket. I moved out of the way as the twins rolled nearer and then spotted that it was my old panda they were fighting over.

'Mine, I believe!' I said, pulling him away from them. 'I had him for my first birthday.'

'You said *I* could have him!' Vicky squealed.

'She didn't, she gave him to me!'

'You hateful pig! He's mine!'

'To save arguments, I'll have him back, then!' Holding him out of reach of their clawing little hands I went through into the hall – and bumped straight into Tim and Jonno on their way in.

'Off for an early night with Teddy?' Jonno said, grinning.

'Ha ha,' I said mirthlessly. 'As a matter of fact, I've just rescued him from the twins.'

'Really? He poked at the poor old panda's stomach, now oozing straw. 'I should say you arrived a bit too late.'

I pushed the stuffing back as best I could. 'You can't have anything in this house,' I said bitterly. 'It's like living in a lunatic asylum.'

Tim and Jonno had followed me into the kitchen. Barry Manilow seemed to be louder in there, probably because he didn't have to compete with the TV.

'Do you share your family's musical taste?' Jonno

asked, motioning upstairs with his head and making a face.

I made an even more gruesome face back. 'You're joking! That's Rachel—she thinks she's sophisticated.'

'Seeing as you're here, kid, how about making a cup of coffee?' Tim said.

'Do you mind! You can make your own coffee—and not so much of the kid.'

'Quite right,' Jonno said. 'What are you — fourteen now?'

'Sixteen!' I said indignantly, and he laughed.

'I was only kidding,' he said, but I don't know whether he was or not. He was all right, Jonno was, but he took his cue from Tim and treated me like *he* did — as a constant source of amusement to have the mickey taken out of on every possible occasion.

Dad put his head round the door. 'How many for fish and chips?' he shouted jovially above Barry Manilow.

Tim looked at Jonno. 'Stopping for some?'

Jonno shook his head. 'Heavy date. Don't want to go out smelling of Chip Shop No. 5.'

Dad disappeared and I reached for the coffee and one mug.

'The lovely Danielle, is it?' Tim asked Jonno, and he nodded.

I put the kettle on. 'Who's Danielle?'

'Someone who goes to college with him,' Tim answered. 'Why, fancy him yourself, do you?'

'Do leave off!' I blustered.

'So what's wrong with me?' Jonno asked, pretending to be hurt. 'I'm good-looking, presentable, I wear no medallions – a girl could do a lot worse.'

'Fancy yourself, don't you?'

Tim made a braying noise. 'She's gone red – she does fancy you! Look out, mate, my kid sister's after you!'

'I am *not*! I haven't gone red, I . . .' But of course I had gone red by then, who wouldn't have? I finished making my coffee and made for the door. 'I'm going upstairs,' I said with as much dignity as I could. 'I've got some homework to do.'

'Don't let us drive you away,' Jonno said.

'It's no good, she can't face it!' Tim said dramatically. 'You're so close, yet you're out of reach. Oh, be still, my heart!'

'Drop dead!' I said rudely to both of them, and stalked out slopping hot coffee over my fingers. Tim was the limit, he really was. They *both* were.

Barry Manilow reached a crescendo as I got to the top of the stairs, wailing that he was going to stand tall and do it his way. I waited for the pause between tracks and then asked Rachel politely if she could turn down the volume.

'I can't,' she said, 'I'm in and out of the bathroom and I want to be able to hear it wherever I go.'

'But I can't hear myself *think*.'

She shrugged, uncaring. She had one of her evening get-ups on and it looked particularly awful; the pink polyester did nothing for her hair. 'Go downstairs, then,' she said.

I gritted my teeth, went into my room and shut the door. Rachel started singing along with the record, putting on an awful husky voice with a fake American accent. Yuk!

Holding what was left of my coffee, I opened the cupboard, climbed over the dolls' house and sat down in the darkness. Bliss! I rested my head against the wall and switched on my torch. How had I come to be in my family? That's what I wanted to know. I was the only one of them who wasn't noisy and loud and untidy.

Maybe there had been a mix-up in the hospital when I'd been born. Maybe Mum had taken the wrong baby home and somewhere there was a nice little quiet house with a nice quiet mum and dad who had a great noisy, riotous sixteen-year-old charging about in it, giving them both heart attacks.

I wondered what Leo was doing. I wanted to read his letter again but I'd left it in the file. Blast! I'd have to clamber out and get it.

It was just as well I did, actually, because no sooner had I emerged than Vicky burst in saying that Dad was back with the fish and chips and I was to go straight down and eat mine.

She bobbed down as she said it and did the fringe-flicking routine.

'Don't keep doing that,' I said irritably. 'It gets on my nerves.'

'Doing what?' she said.

'Bobbing up and down, messing with your hair. It's really aggravating.'

'What's aggravating mean? Anyway, I don't keep doing it.'

'You *do*. It's getting to be like a nervous twitch. You

don't realize you're doing it half the time.'

'Why are you so ratty?' she asked, with interest. She looked at me slyly. 'I expect it's just your age. Mum says when you're ratty it's your age and because you've probably got love problems. *Have* you got love problems?'

'Mind your own business!' Mum had probably meant well but there was nothing more calculated to arouse the twins' curiosity than me having 'love problems'.

'No need to shout. Temper, temper!' She moved out of the door swiftly, before I could reach her. 'I'll tell them you'll be down in a minute, shall I?' When she was half-way down the stairs she added in a low voice, 'when you've worked out what to do about your love problems.'

I clenched my fists; I'd murder her – them – one of these days, really I would.

I found the letter and tucked it in my pocket. I'd hide it in the cupboard with my other treasures as soon as I could, but in the meantime I'd keep it on my person and out of the twins' way.

Love, Leo . . . I remembered how he'd finished the letter and smiled to myself. Did he write that on all his letters, though, just as a matter of course, or did it mean that I was special?

Chapter Three

Monday morning in our house was much the same as it always is. It's a bit like a circus – and Piccadilly Circus at that. The thing is, we all have to be out of the house within ten minutes of each other so there's this more or less constant call of: 'Where's my . . .' 'Has anyone seen . . .' 'I've got to have . . .' and 'For God's sake, you've been in that bathroom for *hours*!'

At least we've got a separate downstairs loo now – it was put in when Mum and Dad bought the house some years ago. Not wishing to be indelicate, but without it life would be impossible.

Mum works as well now; she cleans five mornings a week at a couple of big houses near the common, so she has to be out of the house early, too. It's a scream, really, her being a cleaning lady when our house permanently looks as if a bomb's just dropped, but she says it's different doing someone else's place and she enjoys it. The other thing is that she gets paid, of course, and though Dad works long hours as a lorry driver and gets lots of overtime, I suppose any extra coming in helps with a family as big as ours.

I escaped early that morning and was pleased to be out, savouring the quiet along with the fresh air. As I walked down the path I heard through the open window: 'Come out! You've been in there ages, I want to clean my teeth!' and then an answering: 'I've only just this minute got in, you selfish pig!'

I walked on quickly, heading towards school and

Leo. I'd been looking at his cover ideas at the weekend and come down in favour of a sort of abstract one which made a play on the school's name. Our school is called Waterbridge Comprehensive, named after some old Major Waterbridge who helped found it, so Leo had drawn a shield with water running over it and a bridge spanning the lot. It was quite clever, but I was thinking of asking Jonno if he could improve on it in any way. After all, that was just the sort of thing he was doing at art college.

Laura Crown caught me up. She's in the Sixth too, but not in my tutor group. She's pretty and very popular – and knows it.

'Good weekend?' she said breezily, and waiting for my reply said: 'Mine was. So hectic!'

'Oh yes? I looked at her. She's quite sickeningly pretty – silky dark hair with chestnut streaks and a smooth olive skin.

'Mum's sister came over – she lives up North – with my two cousins. They're both boys and both really good-looking!' She glanced at me sideways for my reaction and I put on a suitably impressed expression.

''Course, they wanted to be taken everywhere, so Friday we went to that new record shop in town – it stays open until ten, and everyone from school was there – and Saturday I took them both to the town hall disco. You should 'have *seen* everyone's faces when I rolled up with not one but *two* good-looking guys!'

'I bet!' I said dutifully.

'And Peter McKnee – well, I've fancied him for ages but never got anywhere – he nearly fell over his jaw when he saw me!'

'You'd better ask them down again,' I said.

'I'm going to! Mind you, I quite fancy Greg myself, he's the older one, but it would be really difficult getting off with one of them, if you see what I mean. I don't know how the other one would react. He might go *mad*.'

'So might Peter McKnee.'

'So he might!' she squealed.

She paused for breath — not for long, though. 'What's this magazine business I've heard about? Aren't you supposed to be doing the editing with Leo?'

I nodded casually. 'It was all his idea — I think he saw a competition for school magazines in one of the Sunday papers and thought it would be a good idea to start one. Good practice for him, too.'

'Oh yes, he wants to be a journalist, doesn't he?'

I nodded again and she looked at me searchingly. 'Fancy him, do you?' I didn't react, not a flicker; she was like my family, always wanting to know everyone's business. 'Because if you do,' she went on, 'you don't stand a chance. Everyone knows he's spoken for.'

I would have loved to have had the strength of will to let this pass but I just couldn't. 'What d'you mean?' I said.

'Well, Tracey lives near him and *she* told me that there's this Tricia girl who's the daughter of his mum's best friend and she's always round there.'

I hesitated, struggling to find some excuse for him. 'So? Perhaps she's no one special. Perhaps she's just delivering messages for her mum.'

'Oh yeah!' Laura gave a harsh laugh. 'You haven't seen her! Tracey says she's got blonde hair right down to her waist and a big bust.'

'Oh,' I said, and swallowed.

'So I should get any ideas about him *right* out of your head.'

'I haven't got any ideas,' I said unconvincingly. 'He's just a friend; someone I happen to be working with on something.'

'Oh yeah – pull the other one!' she said, and I decided, not for the first time, that I didn't really like her.

I told myself repeatedly that morning that I had no need to feel niggled, no need at all. Leo hadn't really given any indication that he fancied me, only to put 'Love, Leo' on his note and say that we made a great team – but he could have written that to anyone.

I saw him at lunchtime: I was in the canteen sitting with Laura and her crowd when he came over. I felt Laura nudge the girl next to her – and then the nudge went on down the line so in the end everyone was looking up at him and straining to hear what he had to say to me.

'Hi, co-editor,' was what he said. 'Had a chance to think about the cover?'

I nodded. His hair was very wild and blond and his eyes very green. Like a lion, he was. Leo the lion, I thought, and grinned.

'What's the joke? You've thought of some new ideas, have you?'

I pulled myself together. 'No . . . sorry, I was just thinking of something else. I . . . er . . . like the bridge and water one best.'

'Mmm. I like that one. I'm not all that good at actually drawing things, though.'

'My brother's got a friend doing graphic design,' I said, well aware of four pairs of eyes on me. 'Maybe he could tidy it up a bit.'

Leo straightened up, ran a hand through his hair. 'That would be great,' he said. 'I want to see you about having a letters page, too. We could let people air their grouses about the school.'

'Good idea!'

'What will it be, £10 for the leading letter like in the newspapers?' Tracy said.

Leo laughed. 'I don't think we can run to that. There'd just be the thrill of seeing your name in print.'

'Oh, big thrill!' Laura said, tossing back her hair and smiling up at him.

'Look, I'll see you at four at the gates,' Leo said to me. 'Maybe we can walk some of the way home together and chat about a few things.'

There were small movements from the line of girls as they all nudged each other again, then Leo walked off and I went back to my lunch – or tried to.

'How about *that*, girls!' Laura said. 'Cool, eh?'

'He'll see her at four and they'll walk home together!' Tracey squeaked. 'I think I'll have a go at this magazine lark.'

'Me, too,' a girl further down the table said. 'He's a bit of all right. What's Mandy got that I haven't?'

'Whatever it is she keeps it well hidden!' Laura said, and they all giggled.

I finished my lunch, my heart thudding away like no one's business, and got up. I felt like creeping off somewhere and having a little think about Leo in private. However, there were no handy cupboards about so it would have to be the school field.

'Let us know how you get on!' Tracey called.

'Bet he kisses good!' someone else said, and I was just thankful that he wasn't within earshot.

Walking round the field didn't stop my heart from racing – in fact, being able to concentrate on Leo made things worse. Suppose he walked me all the way home, I'd *have* to ask him in. Rachel wouldn't be home but Tim would be, and the twins, and Mum in her cleaning overall and the house looking like a tip.

Where would we sit to talk if he did come in? Mum and Tim would be in the kitchen and the table would still have ninety-five varieties of breakfast cereal out on it (we all liked different ones); if we went in the sitting room it would be knee-deep in the twins' toys and most probably the twins themselves. Even if we stood in the hall to chat the twins would come lurching through it forty times to look at Leo or, even worse, keep peering at him round the doors, screeching hysterically.

Maybe I could tell him that he couldn't come in because Mum was ill. No, that was no good: I'd read a Reader's True Story in a magazine only that week where a girl had done exactly that and got caught out. Apparently she'd just started at a posh new school and was ashamed of her mum and dad and where they lived, so she pretended to her new friends that her mum was seriously ill and she couldn't invite people to her home. She'd kept it up for months, had her mum dying of some obscure disease, and then the girls had clubbed together for a bouquet of flowers for poor mum, brought it round to her house – and she'd been well and truly caught out. I didn't want *that* to happen! Anyway, I wasn't ashamed, not really, it was just that Leo wasn't your average boy-next-door, not like the boys I'd grown up with and knocked around with in groups. He was different – and I knew my family would be too much for him all at once. They'd over-whelm him, put him off . . . but if I could just keep them all apart until he and I had got to know each other better, then maybe everything would be all right. They'd have to meet sooner or later – I was going to try and make sure it was later.

Anyway, I reminded myself, what about Tricia with the long blonde hair and the bust? I mustn't think that just because he was walking me home from school she was out of the running.

Leo was waiting outside the school gates for me at going-home time. I'd been to the cloakroom to try and do something with my hair, and applied a touch of lip gloss and a hint of mascara and also borrowed a squirt of perfume from someone, so I was nearly ten minutes late getting out. I crossed the playground and saw him waiting, and got a real kick out of knowing that he was waiting for *me*.

'Sorry I'm late,' I said, suddenly feeling a bit shy. 'I

had a couple of things to do.'

He smiled. 'That's OK — at least everyone else is off home and we'll be able to walk down the road and chat without interruption.' We started walking and he went on: 'A big crowd of your friends just went past and really stared at me for some reason. I began to wonder if I'd grown an extra head or something.'

I hid a smile. 'Was it Laura and that lot?'

He nodded. 'The ones you were sitting with at lunchtime.'

'They're just nosy,' I said.

'I can't stand people like that,' he said. 'I like to keep myself to myself. I hate everyone knowing my business.'

'Me, too,' I said, dying inside. I *couldn't* let my family loose on him! The Roaring Rossiters would pounce on him as soon as he got through the door, bombard him with noise to break down his resistance, demand to know his business and insist that he knew theirs . . .

'Now, about the cover . . .' he said, thankfully changing the subject.

We walked on, talking all the time, and had covered quite a lot of the magazine details by the time we'd reached the railway bridge. I was all for leaving him there, well away from the estate, lovely though it was being with him, but he remembered he wanted to talk about a pop page.

'I'll walk you right home and by then we should have all the basics sorted out,' he said. 'I'd ask you round to my place tonight but my mother's got a bridge party.'

'Oh, that's OK,' I said, my mouth dry. He didn't expect me to ask *him* round instead, did he?

'I think it would be a good idea to get someone to specifically look after the pop,' I said, talking quickly so that we'd be finished before we reached my house. 'They could go through the music papers and pick out unusual bits and do a sort of gossip column.'

'Good idea,' Leo said. His hand, the one not holding the briefcase, swung and touched mine accidentally. I don't know whether his reaction was the same as mine, but to me it felt as if I'd been stung.

'This way?' He nodded towards the traffic lights.

'Yes, but . . . but you needn't come any further. It's so much out of your way,' I said, beginning to panic a little.

'Don't be daft, I'm enjoying it. Walking's supposed to be good for you, isn't it?'

We walked up the High Street, across the green and on to our estate. A few weeks ago the council had been round to paint some of the end walls of the terrace houses which had been covered by graffiti; all I hoped was that no new rude sayings had appeared. I hesitated at the top of Brookdale Road and started to say: 'Well, see you tomorrow' but to my horror he just walked on as if he hadn't heard me.

He was deep in thought. 'We'll need a letters editor,' he said, 'Any of your friends interested or shall I ask Nigel Potter?'

'Er . . . no. Ask Nigel,' I said, my mouth getting drier and drier. 'Are you sure I'm not taking you out of your way?'

'What is all this?' he said, turning to me and smiling. 'Do I look too frail to stand up to a long walk or something?'

'Of course not!' I said hastily.

'Besides, I can double back across the common. Extra fresh air and all that.'

We turned into my road, my legs feeling wobbly. I usually get halfway down and then cross over to the side where we live, but I didn't this time.

We drew near my house. Leo was talking about articles on computers and probably didn't notice that my voice was squeaky when I answered him. We were now *opposite*. I should have crossed over, I nearly did cross, but then I saw that there was a jumble of bikes and skates on the path outside our house which meant that Vicky and Vanessa had friends in. Then I heard a drawn-out 'Mu-um!' from right across the road, so I carried on walking, terrified that any minute one of the twins would come out and yell after me or Tim would pound up and ask me if I'd forgotten where I lived.

No one did, though, and we reached the end of the road. As well as the dry mouth and the wobbly legs I now felt quite sick. What had I done? I'd have to wander about half the night with him now, I couldn't suddenly say I'd walked right past my house without realizing it – not unless I'd suffered a ten-minute memory loss. I quashed an urge to giggle hysterically.

'Across here?' Leo said, indicating the main road, and I nodded. Across anywhere, it didn't matter.

We walked on. I was unable to take in a thing he was saying – and I'm sure I wasn't making any sense in my replies to him. I waited miserably for something to happen so I'd be caught out: for Leo to say, 'You don't live near here, do you?' or for someone from school to come up and drop me right in it, but they didn't.

We reached three houses set some distance back from the road and I saw a possible way out; I couldn't just carry on walking round for hours and hours. I knew the middle house, the Pantiles, because it was one of Mum's cleaning jobs. The owners were out all day so it wouldn't matter if I stood at the top of their drive and pretended that I lived there.

I made up my mind all at once. 'Ah, here we are,' I said to Leo brightly, and I stopped by the stone pillar at the end of the wall.

He glanced towards the house. He didn't say, 'Wow, what a house!' or give an awe-struck whistle, which made me wonder what *his* house was like. 'There, we've got quite a lot sorted out in that twenty minutes,' he said.

Twenty minutes! Just the last four seconds had seemed like twenty hours. 'I . . . I'd better be going in. Lots of homework to do,' I said frantically. I didn't want to rush away, I'd have willingly stayed in his company day and night, but I was just about dying of panic in case the owners suddenly arrived and asked me what I was doing there. Worse, suppose they recognized me. 'Oh look, it's Mandy Rossiter, our char-woman's daughter!' they might call.

'And you're going to ask your brother's friend about the cover?'

I shifted from foot to foot. 'Yeah, sure.' My head

jerked up and down in quick, nervous nods.

'So if we have another chat on Friday, say, we'll both have something actually down on paper.'

'Yes.' Just *go*!

'Maybe you can come round in the evening or something.'

'Lovely. I'll get him to do the cover by then and bring that as well,' I gabbled.

'Well, then . . .'

'Goodbye!' I almost shouted, and I set off at a fair pace down the drive. Please . . . please . . . please just go, I begged him silently. I really like you, but don't suddenly remember something you ought to have told me or stand there watching me.

I glanced round; he was crossing the road opposite the drive. He turned and waved, slowly, casually. He was still in sight – and I was up to the front door of the house.

I stood on the doorstep, half-dead with fright and wondering how I'd got myself into this situation. Suppose there was someone in? Suppose they suddenly flung the door open and sent me packing?

I pretended to ring the bell, just in case he was still watching, then counted to sixty and moved silently away. God, it was awful! I'd tell Sammy about it later and maybe we'd be able to giggle about it, but right then it was *horrific*.

I slunk back up the drive and peered out into the road. There was no sign of him. I had to wait a while, though, to make sure he hadn't gone into one of the shops farther down. I counted to sixty again and then I walked out of the drive as nonchalantly as I could, crossed the road and started towards our estate.

On the way home the significance of what I'd done hit me. At the time I'd have done anything for a quick get-out, anything rather than traipse the streets all night, but by putting off taking him home and ending up there, of all places, I'd just made things worse. It only needed a word from one of the other girls and he'd realize I didn't live in the Pantiles at all. And even if he didn't find out for himself, I couldn't keep walking past my own front door and saying goodbye to him in someone else's driveway.

Oh God, when he found out what I'd done he'd think I was crazy. I *was* crazy; it had to be the stupidest thing I'd ever done.

Miserably, I let myself in at home – and was immediately set upon by Vicky.

'Vanessa said she saw you going by with a boy!' she said, 'Was it really you?'

I clenched my teeth. Those *twins*; they could get a job working for MI.5 any day they liked. 'Might have been,' I said.

Vanessa appeared. 'Why did you go right by?'

'Is his hair bleached, that boy?'

'No, it isn't!'

'So it was you!' Vanessa said. 'Told you it was her.' She pulled a face at Vicky.

'Mummy!' Vicky cried, running into the kitchen to be first with the news. 'Our Mandy's got a boyfriend and he's got bleached hair. She says it's not but it looks as if it is.'

I groaned. Vanessa was still looking at me curiously. 'Why didn't you come in?' she asked. 'Why did you go right by?'

'If you must know, we were going for a walk,' I said. 'Anyway, it's none of your business.'

She pulled a face. '*Be* like that.'

A burst of heavy rock music came out of the sitting room. Tim was in there, obviously.

'I'm going up to do my homework!' I shouted to Mum, but I didn't hear what she said in reply.

Risking the twins, I went into our room and climbed into the cupboard. I wanted to go over everything he'd said while it was still fresh in my mind; I wanted to remember what it had felt like when his hand had brushed mine, and I wanted to think about next Friday.

Most of all, I wanted to work out what I was going to do about the silly, cringe-making mess I'd got myself into.

Chapter Four

'What *have* you got on?' Rachel said to me the following morning. 'Is she allowed to wear those sort of things to school?' she asked Mum, looking critically at my clothes: I was wearing a very short navy skirt and a white blouse which was covered in badges.

'It's not really any of your business, is it?' I said. I'd been awake early worrying about the Pantiles business and I was in no mood for her carping remarks.

'Girls!' Mum said mildly, but I wasn't sure if she was talking to us or the twins – who were fighting over a pop star's picture which had been a free gift in a cereal packet.

'It's mine!'

'It's not! You had it last time!'

'So? It's mine because it's my cereal. Mummy, only the person who eats the cereal can have the picture, can't they?'

'I'm going to eat that cereal too, then!'

'You can't, you pig, Mummy gets it specially for me.'

I looked at my sisters resignedly. When I get married and have children, I'm only having *one*.

'But look at the length of that skirt,' Rachel persisted, 'I can see all your legs. And with those badges you look like a . . . a hippie or something. When I was at school they were very strict about uniform.'

'You were never in the Sixth,' I pointed out. 'We're allowed to show our individuality in the Sixth.'

She sniffed. 'No wonder teenagers today run *wild*.'

'Oh, you'd know all about that, wouldn't you, grannie? I mean, you're still wearing school uniform and you left four years ago. Just look at you!' She was wearing a black pleated skirt, white nylon blouse and navy blue cardigan. Her hair doesn't help matters, I think she's always worn it in the same style: neatly waved, close to the head – it makes her look nearer

46

forty than twenty – and not one of your Jane Fonda trendy forty-year-olds, either. I'm not saying *I'm* terrifically stylish or anything, but she's got absolutely no idea. When she goes out she wears things like a tangerine-coloured jumper with a grey polyester skirt – she's got to be seen to be believed, really she has.

She takes after Mum, of course. Mum's wonderfully frumpy – but then you half expect that in a little, fat forty-five-year-old, don't you? Even Mum's improved, though, since I've got interested in fashion. I often say 'Try your hair like this, Mum,' or point out a dress in a magazine and say it would suit her and sometimes she takes my advice. Rachel, though, is something else.

'My clothes are suitable for my employment,' she said frostily.

'Too true!' I said, spreading honey on my toast. Rachel works as a clerk in local government, putting date stamps on documents all day or something. Anyhow, the job is about as boring as she is. She's got a frumpy friend, too, and in their spare time they go to Barry Manilow appreciation evenings and things like that.

Tim banged his fist on the table and I jumped. 'That's me finished, then!' he said. 'I'm off!'

He beamed round at us and left without taking his plate to the sink – Mum goes mad if we girls don't do it – and rushed up the stairs two at a time for the bathroom. This was a signal for everyone else to jump around shouting: 'Don't be long in there!' 'Oh, I wanted to be first today!' or, if you were a twin, start a fight right in the kitchen doorway so no one could get

47

through. God, what a start to the day.

I saw Laura on the way to school that morning but luckily she didn't see me; I couldn't have faced her probing questions. I've discovered that I really miss not having Sammy at school. Although I get on all right with people like Laura, without a best friend around it just isn't the same. And it's too late now to make another best friend, of course. They don't just grow on trees.

I couldn't avoid everyone or stop the questions at lunchtime, though.

'Come and sit with us and tell us all about lovely Leo!' Laura called across the canteen to me.

'Yeah, and we want to hear *everything*. All the juicy bits!' Tracey said.

I felt myself going red. I hate the way they want to know each little detail. I mean, even in the unlikely event that Leo had grabbed me and smothered me with passionate kisses I'd hardly want it broadcast round the school.

'I keep telling you, I'm just working on the magazine with him,' I said, sitting down at their table with my lunch of pork pie and tomato.

'And I keep telling you to pull the other one!' Laura said, and they both laughed.

'So what happened?'

'He just walked home with me and we talked about the magazine,' I said. 'That's all.'

'What, no sneaky little kisses going across the green?' Tracey wanted to know.

I sighed. 'You're as bad as my sisters,' I said, 'and if

you must know – no, there weren't.'

'There,' she said with satisfaction. 'I *knew* he wouldn't. He's too mixed up with that Tricia girl.' She hesitated, then asked, 'Laura told you about Tricia, did she?' She sounded so smug about it I got the feeling that if there hadn't been a Tricia she would have invented one.

'Yes, thanks,' I said smoothly. I nonchalantly cut the pork pie into quarters, the tomato into half. I wasn't going to let them see I was bothered, not for *anything* was I.

'She's really something to look at. Never went to school round here; always went to private ones.'

The tomato squirted as I bit into it – and just at that moment Leo walked into the canteen, spotted me and waved.

'Mandy! You're covered in tomato pips!' Laura screeched.

'All down your chin – I hope Leo didn't see,' Tracey added.

I tried to ignore them. Leo was with Nigel and there weren't two spaces on our table so they went across to the other side of the canteen. He smiled and said hello as he passed. I was dead pleased he couldn't sit with us – not with Laura and Tracey nudging each other to death with every remark he addressed to me. Anyway, somehow I had to clear up with him the little matter of my not living at the Pantiles, before we were together in company. Just imagine the field day Laura and Tracey would have if *that* somehow came out in conversation.

I hung about at four o'clock so that I was late coming out of school — just in case Leo was waiting for me. I didn't think he would be, I was just playing safe. I couldn't have stood another walk home like the one the day before, I'd have been dead of fright before we got there.

I went round to see Sammy after supper and told her about the whole incident.

'Suppose someone had come out of the house!' she said, her eyes wide with horror and disbelief. 'Suppose they'd said in a loud voice: "Oh, it's the cleaning woman's daughter!"'

'I know!' I said, pulling an equally anguished face. 'And what am I going to do *now*?'

'*God* knows!' She paused in the middle of doing her make-up. It wasn't too elaborate because she was only going to watch Graham at football practice. 'Maybe you could say that you've moved. Moved very quickly.'

'Oh yes,' I said. 'It's very likely we've moved from the Pantiles to a council estate. Very likely indeed.'

She lipbrushed her mouth into a perfect line and then turned and beamed at me. 'I know! You could say you were only going there to leave a message for your mum. You forgot to mention that you didn't actually *live* there yourself.'

'I can't do that!'

'OK, then,' she shrugged. 'Tell him the truth — that your house is too untidy and your family are too awful and noisy and you wanted him to think you lived somewhere posh.'

'How *can* I?' I wailed.

'The choice is yours!' she said, waving a great big fat blusher brush in the air. She got up from her stool and walked up and down the centre of the room like a cat-walk model. 'How do I look?'

'Great,' I said. She had on a straight black skirt with a slit up the back and a top made of sweatshirt material with a loose cowl neckline. 'Very slinky. A bit much for football practice though, perhaps.'

'We'll go in the Centre afterwards for a coke. If I'm lucky,' she added. 'And now I really must drive you away, I've got to be at the ground at seven-thirty.'

I rolled my eyes but didn't say anything. He didn't even come and collect her!

Sammy and I left together – she went to catch the bus at the end of the road, wiggling her bottom in her straight skirt; I walked home, deep in thought.

When I got in, Jonno was in the hall talking to Tim; a piece of motorbike, don't ask me what sort of piece, was on the floor between them.

'Hello, gorgeous! Jonno said to me, and he put out a hand to ruffle my hair. I ducked away from him, trying to look annoyed – but actually I didn't much mind. 'Before you go,' I said, 'I wanted to ask you about the cover for our school mag.'

'Fire away, sweetheart,' he said in an old-American-movie voice. 'Tim and I have settled our business; I was just leaving.'

'I'll go and get the bike started,' Tim said, picking up the piece of whatever-it-was and heading for the garage. 'Thanks, mate.'

'If you just hang on a sec,' I said to Jonno, 'I'll go and get the magazine cover stuff.'

I dashed upstairs, clambering over the 'going-up' pile: a roller boot, a teddy nightdress case, six books, a pair of curtains and a lot of Vicky's badly cut-out kitten pictures; it was just as well that Jonno was used to us and all our mess, I thought.

'Here it is,' I said, bringing down the cover in its plastic case and handing it to him. 'I . . . we . . . just wondered if you could make it a bit sharper or something.'

He looked at it consideringly for some time and I looked at *him*. He was, when you stood back and regarded him in a detached way, actually quite good-looking. He had very soft dark hair, long eye-lashes, high cheek-bones and . . .

Vicky came out of the sitting room and just stood there staring at me. Mum shouted: 'Is that you, dear? and Vicky said it was.

'I can do something with this,' Jonno said, 'you'll have to let me start again from scratch, though.'

'That'll be OK,' I said. 'Whatever you want.'

Vanessa appeared and stood next to Vicky. 'I thought you were out here talking to your boyfriend,' she said baldly.

'Well I'm not, so you can go away,' I said. Upstairs Barry Manilow had begun singing about love and pain and all that and the twins both contorted their faces in an exaggerated way and started groaning. Jonno laughed; I just looked at them coldly.

'When d'you want it back by?' he asked.

'Well, I'm seeing Leo on Friday, could I have it by then?'

Jonno grinned at me. He's got blue eyes, very sparkly. 'Ah, Leo is the love interest, is he?'

The twins didn't say anything but I felt them stiffen and become alert. I looked away from Jonno to glower at them.

'Can't you just clear off!' I said. 'This is a private conversation.'

'Ooh, aren't you the nasty one!' Vanessa said, pulling a face.

'Must be her *love problems*!' Vicky shrieked, and I moved to shove them back inside the sitting room but, wonder of wonders, they disappeared of their own accord, giggling hysterically.

'Sorry about them,' I said to Jonno.

'So ... er ... Leo?'

'He's not my boyfriend or anything,' I said quickly. 'Not really.'

'Oh yeah, I forgot. You're too young for all that!'

'No, I'm not!' I said indignantly, thinking I'd rather be teased about having a boyfriend than as being too young to get one.

'Caught you!' he said. 'I knew from the way you blushed when you said his name that there was something in it.'

'There isn't,' I insisted. 'Not yet.' I had a sudden longing to tell all – to ask his advice about what to do, but I didn't dare. He'd probably tell Tim – and anyway the twins were just the other side of the sitting-room door, more than likely with their ears pressed to it.

'It's OK, I won't pry,' he said. He folded the cover. 'You don't mind, do you – only I've got to start again from the beginning anyway.'

I shook my head, he put the cover in his inside pocket and pulled out a small box. 'What d'you think of this?' he said. 'It's for someone's birthday.'

He smiled at me as he said it and the situation reminded me a bit of those stories – you know, where the hero says he's bought a diamond ring and the heroine has to be all coy and pretend she doesn't know it's for her but she does *really* – and then I felt all embarrassed when I thought that and couldn't look at Jonno. As if he'd be buying *me* presents.

He lifted the lid: it was a coiled gold chain, very thick and slinky.

'What d'you think?' he asked, lifting it out and letting it swing in the air so the light caught it and made it sparkle.

'It's lovely,' I said.

'It doesn't look as if it's got something missing, does it?'

'What d'you mean?'

'Well, I showed my mother and she asked me where the locket had got to. She thinks it's funny to have a chain with nothing on it.'

I shook my head. 'Of course it isn't. Everyone has plain gold chains.'

'So you think she'll like it?'

'It's for Danielle?' I asked, and he nodded.

'It's hell getting presents for girls – Danielle's quite fussy about what she does and doesn't like. She wanted a chain but it had to be real gold and thick and she wanted it smooth, not a rope type.'

'Oh,' I said. It seemed to me that it was enough to say what present you wanted without specifying that it had to be thick and smooth and gold, as well. 'It's lovely,' I said. 'It looks really expensive.'

'Good!' He put the lid back on the box. 'Danielle likes expensive-looking things.'

I nodded understandingly, but thought to myself that I didn't much like the sound of her. She was probably what Mum called a 'gold-digger'.

'I'll bring this back as soon as I've done it,' he said, patting his pocket.

'Before Friday!' I reminded him.

'Of course. You won't have to let lover-boy down.' He ruffled my hair again. 'Goodbye kid!' he said, and left.

I took a step towards the sitting-room door, opened it – and fell over Vicky and Vanessa. They collapsed, giggling.

'Who's lover boy?' Vicky said between giggles.

'Is it that boy with bleached hair?'

'Mum!' I protested. 'They've been listening at the door!'

Mum laughed. 'They don't mean any harm; it's just their idea of fun!'

I made an angry growling noise at them – which only made them giggle harder – and went upstairs. Bravely edging past Barry Manilow, I went into the bedroom and got into my cupboard.

I sat there for a few minutes, just letting the darkness and silence wash over me and not thinking about anything in particular — and then my number one problem surfaced and hit me and I started rehearsing what I was going to say to Leo.

'Oh, by the way, Leo,' I muttered quietly in the dark, 'You know when you walked me home the other day, well as a matter of fact I don't actually live where you left me . . .'

Or maybe it should be: 'Super house where my mum works, wasn't it, Leo? You know, where you left me the other day . . .'

Or then again: 'I had a message to deliver to my mum the other evening — oh, I forgot, you were with me, weren't you? — she works in that big house you left me at, didn't I say?'

But why on earth should anyone have a message to deliver to their own mum straight from school? I bit my lip and sighed despairingly. How *was* I going to get out of it? He'd think I was a complete ninny when I told him; he'd *never* ask me out. It was all their fault of course: the family's. If they hadn't been like they were, I would have brought Leo home without even thinking about it. It was because of them that everything was ruined.

I sat there for fifteen minutes or so rehearsing things to say and not getting anywhere, and then I heard someone coming up the stairs so I quickly climbed out and stretched myself along my bed.

Vicky crashed the door open. 'Mummy says if you

haven't got any homework could you go and give her a hand with the ironing,' she reported. She looked round for evidence of books. 'You haven't got any homework, have you?' She bobbed down to the floor, flicked and bobbed up again.

'No,' I said shortly.

'Well, then . . .'

'It's OK, I'm coming,' I groaned, and got up and went downstairs. I hate ironing but we all have to take turns helping with it – except Tim, of course.

It was while I was ironing that I remembered I hadn't even *started* worrying about Friday. I would be at Leo's house with his mum and she'd probably be madly posh and I'd do everything wrong and feel small and insignificant and . . . I stopped ironing for a moment, horror-struck: suppose he'd told his mum that I lived at the Pantiles and she had friends next door or something! Worse, suppose she knew the people who lived there!

'Mind that dress, dear,' Mum said, busily folding sheets on the other side of the room. I snatched up the iron and realized I'd made the hem of one of Rachel's polyester numbers all funny and wavy by keeping the heat on it for too long.

I licked my fingers and patted the offending patch. She probably wouldn't notice.

I sighed. They say that being in love makes you absent-minded, don't they? Perhaps I really was, then . . .

Chapter Five

'You're coming round tonight, aren't you?' Leo asked me, as we met outside the school gates at four o'clock. 'Do you want me to meet you somewhere?'

It was Friday. I was going to his house that very evening – and I still hadn't said anything to him about not living at the Pantiles. I'd been torn two ways all week; on the one hand dying to see him and talk to him, but instead going out of my way to avoid him in case the subject came up.

'I don't mind,' I said, shrugging in what I hoped was a carefree way. If he said he'd come round for me I was going to faint on the spot.

'Do you know where I live?'

'I think so.' Of course I knew, I'd looked him up in the telephone directory earlier in the week. Everyone knew Elstree Crescent because it was just about the nicest road on Hurst Green and the only one with flowering cherry trees along each side of it. Families from other districts came in their cars each spring just to see the blossom.

'Well, if you're not sure, I could come round for you – or meet you in the High Street if you like.'

'Oh, the High Street would be fine!' I said with relief. It was only a one-second feeling of relief, though. I *had* to tell him.

He turned away. 'See you tonight, then. Outside the big dry cleaners?'

'Fine!' My heart was in my mouth. 'Oh, just a sec!'

He looked at me enquiringly.

'The cover looks good,' I improvised quickly. 'My brother's friend gave it back last night.'

'That was quick work.'

'He's very keen. He's super on design stuff.'

'Great. I'll see it tonight, then.'

'Just a minute,' I croaked urgently. 'There's something I wanted to say.'

Four second-year girls went by and looked at us. 'Wish I had a boyfriend,' I heard one say wistfully, but I was too worried about what I had to say to begin a new worry about whether Leo had heard or not.

'You know . . . well, you're going to think I'm quite mad,' I began breathlessly, 'but you know on Monday when you walked home with me I . . . we . . . didn't walk to my house.'

He screwed his nose up. I noticed that he had six very pale gold freckles on it and they'd merged into each other. 'We didn't?' he said, clearly mystified. 'Why didn't we?'

I felt a bit better; at least no one had already told him. I crossed my fingers behind my back. 'Well, I . . . I had to go and see my mum for something so I went to where she works, only I felt daft saying that she . . . she cleans there so I didn't. Say, I mean.' I let out my breath in a sigh of relief, 'There, I've told you.'

'I still can't see why . . .'

'I was just a bit nervous, I suppose,' I explained. 'It was the first time we'd walked home together and everything. I mean, I wouldn't want you to think I was a snob or anything not admitting my mum's a cleaner, it wasn't that, it was just that I was embarrassed and just let you sort of presume I lived there.'

He grinned and shrugged. 'It's OK. It doesn't really matter, does it?'

'Not really,' I said in relief.

'So where do you live?'

'On the Parkview Estate. One of the big houses.' I paused and then thought I might as well give him the complete shock. 'There are seven of us, you see. Five children.'

I waited for a look of agonized disbelief to cross his face but it didn't. 'I don't know where that is exactly so I'll still meet you in the High Street, shall I?' he said, and I nodded.

'Seven o'clock?'

I nodded again. 'See you!'

I walked off weak with relief. Thank *God* I'd managed to get it out at last. I'd said it all wrong, of course, got too embarrassed and gabbly about it and so made too much of it, but at least I'd got it off my conscience.

I walked home happier than I had been for days; I'd got *that* silly business all cleared up and I had a date, well, an almost-date, with the best-looking, nicest guy in the Sixth. All I had to do now was to keep him and my family apart for as long as possible.

The only other fly in the ointment was this Tricia person — but maybe it was just a friendly thing, like Jonno and me. If their mums were close they couldn't help but be thrown together. And he was so nice to me, looked at me as if I was special, winked at me across the canteen . . . he wouldn't do all that unless he really thought a lot of me, surely he wouldn't.

When I got in I did some homework and then Mum called us down for tea. It was a nice big salad with cold meat. I carefully lifted out the sliced onion which had been placed amongst the lettuce. Just in case — you know . . .

'I'm going out tonight,' I announced to Mum. Dad was on a long run and wouldn't be in until late.

Tim and Rachel didn't take much notice but Vicky and Vanessa looked at me eagerly.

'With a boy?' Vanessa asked.

I ignored her. 'I'm going round to someone's house to talk about the school magazine,' I said to Mum.

'All right, dear. Don't be too late.'

'Is he bringing you home? Can we wait up and see him?' Vicky said.

I carried on with my meal, ignoring them, looking carefully at the potato salad and hoping there wasn't any onion lurking in it.

'As you're going out can I borrow your cassette recorder?' Rachel said. 'Michelle's got a new American concert tape — I can play it on mine and record it on yours.'

'If you like,' I said. I was feeling generous. 'Remember you owe me a favour, then.'

'Really,' she tutted, 'can't you do anything for someone without expecting repayment?'

'No,' I said.

'Well, you won't get far with *that* attitude.' She pursed her lips, an awful orange colour they were.

'You wait until you get out into the real world, you'll soon get your come-uppance.'

'I am in the real world.'

'You're still at school!' she said witheringly. 'When you get a job you'll find things are very different.'

I crunched some potato salad – there *was* onion in it. 'I thought you were asking me for my cassette recorder,' I said, 'not delivering a lecture.'

She nodded wisely. 'Just giving you a few pointers.'

I looked at her; she thinks she knows everything, she really does. Out of all of them, I think I like her the least. I know it sounds awful to say that about one's sister, but really we just aren't alike in any way. She's always treated me as if I'm a small, insignificant insect she'd quite like to tread on.

After tea I helped Mum wash up and then went upstairs and cleaned my teeth, twice. I looked in the bathroom cabinet to see if there were any of those little sprays you squirt down your throat, but there weren't. I huffed into my cupped hands; I didn't *think* I could smell onion.

I washed and changed into the green dress I'd chosen – one that Mum says I look 'sweet' in. I'd almost stopped wearing this particular dress since Mum had said that, but I'd decided to put it on because I was out to make an impression on Leo's mum. I was quite sure she would be frightfully well-dressed and elegant. I put just a little eye make-up on and only lip-glossed my lips. Just in case . . .

'I'm going now!' I shouted to Mum, and slipped out before Vicky and Vanessa could cross-examine me.

Tim and Jonno were working in the garage as I passed.

'Oh, it's a little walking pea pod!' Tim said, making me wonder immediately if I had time to go back and change.

'Not a pea pod,' Jonno said, 'she looks more like a tree. A nice little willow tree.'

I couldn't make up my mind whether it was nice to be called a willow tree or not so I just made a face at him. 'Thanks for the cover,' I said. 'Tim gave it to me this morning.'

'You liked it?'

I nodded. 'Smashing.' I patted my folder. 'I've got it here all ready for Leo to see.'

'Well, if you want anything else done let me know.'

'Thanks.' I went to walk away, then remembered. 'Did she like the gold chain?'

'Danielle? Yeah, I think so.'

I looked at him, puzzled.

'Well, she said she did. I suppose she did. She's not really the sort of girl to rave on about presents.'

'No?' I said. What an old whatsit *she* sounded.

He grinned. 'Have a good evening, anyway.'

'Don't do anything we wouldn't!' Tim bellowed as I walked down the road.

I walked slowly because I was early. I felt dead nervous so I took some Yoga-type deep breaths that one of the gym teachers had told us were good for stress.

I had got as far as the Green, when I had the strangest feeling that I was being followed. I looked round sharply, wondering if I was getting some sort of complex – but there was no one there.

I walked on, crossed the road by the traffic lights – and caught a glimpse of someone out of the corner of my eye. I looked round quickly – just in time to see a small figure dodge behind a wall.

It couldn't be . . . I'd *kill* them! I marched back to the wall and heard muffled giggles even before I'd got there.

'Come OUT!' I shouted.

'We were just . . . were just . . .' the giggles increased in volume.

'We were just going for a walk!' Vanessa burst out.

'You were following me, you little beasts!'

'It was Vicky's idea. She wanted to see your boy-friend.'

Vicky fixed her large, innocent gaze on me, bobbed her head and flicked the fringe back out of her eyes. 'It *wasn't* my idea,' she said earnestly. 'I didn't even *think* of it.'

'Ooh, you liar!'

'I'm not. You made me come.'

'I did *not*!'

'You did!'

'You are both disgusting, horrible little sneaks,' I said in the coldest, most haughty tone I could summon up, 'and if you don't clear off home this minute I'm going to knock both your heads together.'

They cleared off – and I stamped down the road, absolutely furious. My anger stayed with me all the way to the High Street so that I forgot my Yoga breaths and forgot to walk slowly – but Leo was already there, waiting by the dry cleaners where we'd arranged. He smiled and began to walk towards me and the scummy old mood I was in began to disperse almost immediately. My family couldn't touch me *now*.

'Got everything?' he asked.

I said hello and nodded at the same time.

'Great. It won't take long to get everything done. We can go out for a coffee afterwards, maybe. Or a walk or something.'

'Fine.' I fell happily into step beside him, feeling great. He must like me or he wouldn't have suggested a walk.

His house was lovely, of course: glossy-magazine smart, everything looking new and shiny, with carpets thick enough to catch your feet in and big, squashy settees in pale pastel colours.

We sat together at a polished table in the dining room and went over the contents page and the pop section, the letters page, the software reviews, the Waterbridge gossip column and the other features, agreeing on most things, arguing a bit about others. Sometimes he'd be bent over a page, puzzling over something and chewing his pen, and my thoughts would start to wander and I'd think distracting things like: what would it be like if he kissed me? And then I had to hurriedly pull myself together before he looked up and saw me staring.

About nine-thirty there was a noise in the hall and a woman's voice called: 'I'm home, darling!'

'My mother,' Leo said. He looked at his watch, 'Her class must have finished early.'

'Oh,' I said. I ran my tongue nervously across my lips, pushed a few stray pieces of hair behind my ears. I'd expected his mother to be in, been awfully relieved when she wasn't, and hoped to be gone by the time she arrived home – but now I'd obviously have to face her.

'Hello!' A woman walked in and I did a double-take. She was wearing stretch-velvet jeans and a baggy top and at first glance looked to be in her twenties.

'Hello,' I said nervously.

'Oh Ma, this is Mandy,' Leo said.

She turned a sparkly smile on me. 'How's it going? Super idea to do the mag, isn't it?'

I nodded, still dumbstruck. She didn't look at all like a mum. Not my mum, any rate.

'I hope Leo's made you coffee,' she said. 'I left the percolator full.'

'No, it's OK,' I said awkwardly. 'I haven't been thirsty.'

'Coffee's not for when you're thirsty!' she said. 'Coffee gets you going again when you're flagging!'

I smiled politely.

'I'll leave you two workaholics to it! I'm going to practise what I've learnt tonight.' And she went out, leaving a subtle trace of expensive perfume behind her.

I looked at Leo, half-expecting him to appear as stunned as I was by the appearance of this exotic creature.

'What class does she go to?' I asked timidly.

'Friday . . .' Leo said, counting on his fingers,

66

'Friday is flower arrangement evening. The Japanese sort.'

'Oh,' I said. One exotic lotus blossom placed in a container with a thin black twig. That figured.

We pressed on; the magazine was looking pretty good. I'd only gone into it initially because of Leo but I really felt quite enthusiastic all of a sudden. It would be nice, too, to have a name around the school, to be known as one of the magazine editors, someone to be reckoned with.

It was gone ten o'clock when Leo's mother (she was a definite 'mother', not a mum) put her head round the door again. 'Still hard at it? *Do* stop and have coffee.'

Leo looked at his watch. 'Look at the time! We were going out, weren't we, but there's not really any time now.'

I shook my head. 'I really ought to be going soon,' I said, still wondering whether he was going to take me home or not.

'Two coffees coming up!' his mother said gaily. 'Do come through!'

Leo winked at me when she'd gone back to the kitchen. 'She'll be disappointed if we don't. She likes to chat to my friends.'

I started collecting up the various pages. He hadn't said *girlfriends*, but I didn't know whether to be pleased about that or not.

The kitchen was quite unlike ours. It was tidy, for a start, and everything was pine – a pine which shone with a satiny glow. The worktops were made of tiny little brown tiles; in our kitchen the worktops are just ordinary white surfaces but you never see them anyway because they're covered in about four thousand bits and pieces.

I sipped at the coffee while Leo's mother chatted to me just as if I was a friend of hers. I felt strangely awkward, though. She was really nice, yet occasionally I felt she was putting me down. When I said there were seven of us, for instance, she gave a little scream of horror. 'Your poor mother!' she said. 'Still, I expect she's got help around the house.'

I swallowed. 'No,' I said, 'not unless you count *us* as helpers.' I didn't look at Leo; I suppose I should have just said casually that she was a cleaning lady herself actually, but I couldn't bring myself to do so. A little while after that she asked what Dad did and when I said he was a lorry driver she just raised her eyebrows.

I finished my coffee at last – deciding that percolated coffee was bitter and I preferred instant any time – and stood up.

'I'd better be off,' I said. 'Mum doesn't really like me walking through the estate on my own.'

'Parkview Estate?' she asked, and when I nodded I thought I saw the eyebrows lift again.

'You won't be on your own, silly, I'll walk you back,' Leo said, and I smiled at him gratefully.

His mother saw us to the door. As we passed the telephone (pale yellow, press-button type) on the hall table she gave a cry of horror.

'Darling! I quite forgot – Tricia rang you this afternoon about tickets for her college disco. She's got to let them know by Monday apparently.'

I felt myself go cold all over. I put my hands in the pockets of my 'sweet' green dress and clenched my fists.

'Oh, I'll ring her sometime over the weekend,' Leo said as I turned to say my goodbyes.

'Goodbye dear!' his mother called from the step, then: 'Straight back, Leo!'

'Mothers!' he said as we walked down the road. 'She still thinks I'm ten years old.'

I smiled politely. She didn't like me, I knew she didn't.

'She's really attractive,' I said, hoping my voice didn't sound hollow. 'She looks really young.'

'Oh, she'd love to hear you say that,' Leo said. 'She was only eighteen when she had my brother. When we're all out together she likes people to think she's our older sister.'

At the High Street he stopped dead. 'Now, which way?' he said. 'You're not taking me off to any strange houses to meet your mother at this time of night, are you?'

'Of course not,' I said, blushing in the darkness.

'I'm only teasing! I know the way really,' he said, and started walking towards our estate.

I began to feel uneasy, wondering who would still be up when he got to my house. Even more, wondering if he was going to kiss me or anything. Suppose Tim and Jonno were still working on something in the garage when we got outside? Suppose he went to kiss me and the up-and-over door rolled up and there they were grinning at us?

Surely he wouldn't kiss me, though. I mean, he'd made no overtures at all, hadn't even put his arm round me. I didn't even know if I was 'going out' with him. And what about stupid old Tricia? We crossed the road and I adjusted the file of papers under my arm.

'OK with those?'

'Sure. They're not heavy.'

As my left hand came back from doing the adjustment Leo took it and held onto it. It was so unexpected and I was so taken aback that I couldn't speak for a moment. This was it, surely. This was something, was Highly Significant.

By the time we reached my road my hand felt kind of clammy in his but I was scared to shift it in case he thought I wanted to let go.

'I live halfway down here. By the lamp post.'

He nodded. 'When are we going to see each other again?'

My hand suddenly felt even clammier. 'Monday at school?' I suggested. I was playing the story heroine part now and pretending not to know what he really meant.

'No. Properly. I meant in the evening or something.'

'Oh!' I tried to look surprised. 'I don't know; any evening you like.'

'I'll think of somewhere to go and we'll talk about it at school on Monday if you like.'

'OK. Fine.' A whole weekend. A whole weekend to wait until I knew exactly when the date was. Two whole days when he could be seeing Tricia. We reached my house and I stopped. 'Here's where I live.'

'Right.'

I smiled at him, one ear straining to hear if there was anyone still in the garage, my eyes flickering to the upstairs windows for signs of Vicky and Vanessa.

'Goodnight, then.' The hand holding mine slid up my arm and grasped it tightly. I bent forward slightly and was just about to close my eyes when there was a gentle squeal of brakes and a car drew up beside us. I stood there blinking in the headlights, unable to see a thing.

'Be a love and open the garage door, Mandy!' my dad called from the driver's seat.

I shot a look at Leo, sighed – and went to do as he asked. We stood there awkwardly, shuffling our feet, while Dad drove the car in. I thought I would introduce them when Dad came out but he started rooting around in the back of the car obviously looking for something, leaving Leo and I just staring at each other and not knowing what to do.

'Well, I'll see you Monday,' I said uncertainly.

'Yes. Sure.' He smiled, squeezed my shoulder – and then turned and walked away.

Feeling indignant, cross and cheated, I went in. He'd held my hand, we'd almost got a date fixed up – one more minute and he would have kissed me. My family had spoilt it all again . . .

Chapter Six

'What's this?' Vicky said, picking up my school rough book from the hall table the next day. 'Who is Leo Mann and why is his name written all over your book?'

'Give that to me!'

'And there's all hearts and things,' she went on, holding it at arm's length. And your name written inside a ring with his and – ouch!'

I'd grabbed the book back and had somehow managed to scratch her hand.

'Mummy! Mandy's scratched me!' She burst into piteous false sobs. 'Scratched all my hand!'

'Well you shouldn't be so blasted nosy!' I said. 'Keep your hands off my things.'

'It was on the table. *I* didn't know it was private. How am I supposed to know these things, I just . . .'

'Oh, do shut up!'

'Mummy!' The wails increased. Vanessa came out of the kitchen and looked at her with interest.

'Did Mandy hit you?'

'A big scratch. All down my arm. *And* she told me to shut up.'

I glowered at her and moved to go upstairs to do some homework.

'I'm sure Mandy didn't mean it!' Mum's voice sailed through from the kitchen soothingly. She never takes sides, I'll say that for her. Always sits on the fence.

'She did! She . . .'

The phone in the hall rang and I hesitated in case it

was Sammy for me. Vicky stopped wailing as if someone had turned her sound off and picked up the receiver. 'Forbury five two three five,' she said. She always says it so fast that no one can make out what the number is.

'I *said* five two three five,' she repeated, just as fast.

I came down the stairs again.

'Give it to me,' I ordered her.

She glared at me. 'Who *is* it please?' she said officiously into the phone. 'Who is calling?'

'Oh.' Her voice suddenly went all different, all high and silly. 'Oh, I'll just get her. It's Leo, you say? And you want Mandy?'

I snatched the phone away.

'Oh-ow! My hand!' she screeched. 'My same hand!'

I turned my back on her.

'Who is it?' I heard Vanessa ask excitedly. 'Is it her boyfriend?'

'She hurt me. She really hurt me. I'm going to tell Mummy.'

They went into the kitchen and I took a deep breath to calm myself.

'Er. Hello?' I said.

'Mandy?'

A blast of Lionel Ritchie came down the stairs from Rachel's room. I put my hand over my left ear and pressed the receiver hard to my right. 'Yes. It's me.'

'It's Leo.'

'Yes. Hi!'

The kitchen door opened again and Vicky and Vanessa stood in the doorway. Mum was making the usual Saturday soup, liquidizing it in the blender from which there was issuing a great mechanical roar.

'Close the door!' I hissed.

'What?'

'Sorry. Not you,' I said to Leo.

'Mummy says she's going to speak to you about you scratching me.'

'There's a mark there!' Vanessa put in eagerly.

'Shut *up!*'

'Are you still there?' Leo said, sounding bewildered.

'Er . . . sorry. My sisters are playing up,' I explained.

'They sound a bit of a handful.'

'More like a sackful!' I glared at the two of them, then indicated with my head that they should clear off. They didn't move. I turned my back on them again.

Mum came out of the kitchen. 'Mandy, could you . . . oh, you're on the phone,' she said.

I shot her an agonized look.

'Sorry, dear,' she said brightly, and went back in the kitchen.

'Mandy, are you still with me?'

'Yes. Sorry.' I could feel myself getting hotter and hotter. 'Lots of . . . er . . . distractions this end.'

I pulled the telephone cord to its entire length and moved inside the sitting room. The wire was just long enough to get the receiver and me through the door, the other bit had to hang outside strung tightly across the hall.

'I just wondered how you got on last night.'

'Last night?' I wasn't really with him. Not surprisgly.

'Your father. I thought he might have had a go at you for being late or being outside with me when he came in or something. I know some fathers are funny about their daughters.'

I found myself frowning into the receiver. How many fathers with daughters did he know then? 'No. He didn't say anything,' I said. 'He stayed out in the garage for ages, actually. I was in bed by the time he came in.'

'That's OK, then. It was all a bit awkward, wasn't it?'

'Saying goodnight?' I could feel my hands beginning to go clammy. 'It was a bit.'

'Mmm. I mean, I thought we were . . . well, I was just about to kiss you goodnight, actually.'

There was a silence; I held my breath. 'Were you?' I whispered.

'Yes. And then everything got messed up and I had to leave you all abruptly. I felt a bit rotten about it.'

I breathed out, very gently. 'It's OK. It wasn't your fault.'

'Next time, then.'

'Next time . . .' I echoed in a croaky voice.

There was another long silence and I felt very breathless and very close to him, then suddenly the noises from the hall and elsewhere in the house began to intrude. 'I'd better go,' I said. I wanted to preserve this magic moment, carry it upstairs carefully before something happened to spoil it. 'The twins are going to burst in here in a minute.'

'Your sisters? I didn't know they were twins.'

'Sometimes they seem more like quads,' I said darkly.

There was a sudden roar of outrage from the hall and the receiver was jerked out of my hand and crashed onto the floor. 'Who left the telephone wire stretched across the hall?' Dad bellowed.

I put my head outside the door hastily. 'Sorry, Dad. I'll explain in a minute.' I picked up the receiver, 'Sorry,' I said again. 'A small catastrophe.'

'That's OK.' He sounded bemused.

'I . . . I'll see you Monday, then.' Unless you can't live another moment without seeing me and are going to ask me out tonight . . .

'Yes. Monday. Goodbye, then.'

'Goodbye, Leo,' I said softly hoping it sounded like I meant it to sound: all soft and intimate.

Carrying the telephone, I went cautiously into the hall. Dad had vanished but Vicky and Vanessa were there, sitting on the stairs like a couple of puppets and grinning the same identical grins.

'Goodbye, darling!' Vanessa cried dramatically.

'Goodbye, my angel. Until we meet again!'

'Oh, I can't live without you another moment!'

'Oh, sweet one, I . . .'

'Shut UP!' I shouted, and pushed through them to go upstairs and shut the bedroom door on them and try and think wonderful thoughts.

What actually happened was that I spent most of the weekend thinking about Tricia and wondering what she looked like. The more I agonized, the better she

76

got. She was Miss World with a fantastic bust — like Dolly Parton's — and long blonde hair like Jerry Hall's by the time I'd finished with her. As soon as I got on a proper footing with Leo, I decided, I'd ask him exactly who she was and what she was to him. I had to know.

Sunday night Tim brought a girl home so there were eight of us sitting around in the living room watching TV. The twins were on cushions on the floor, Mum, Dad and Rachel were on the settee, I was in one armchair and Tim and this Carol girl were together in another.

Honestly, Tim and Carol just didn't care. Their chair was set back a bit from everyone else's and every now and then out of the corner of my eye I could see them kissing each other. The twins were beside themselves; *I* thought it was awful. Tim had been seeing her for ages, though, on and off, so I suppose she was used to him and just didn't see anything wrong in it. She was certainly used to *us*, calling Mum and Dad by their Christian names, Tom and Ida, and generally looking completely at home sprawled around the place in old, tight jeans and Tim's tee-shirts. I don't think it ever crossed *her* mind that maybe she ought to cut down on the make-up or wear demure dresses to gain Mum's approval.

About eight-thirty, just as Mum was telling the twins for the fortieth time to go and get ready for bed, there was a knock on the door.

'I'll go!' I said. I didn't think it *was* him, but I'd come to the conclusion that it didn't do to take chances. Not in our house.

It was Jonno. 'Tim in?' he said hopefully.

I nodded. 'In the sitting room. With Carol.'

Jonno's face fell. 'Oh, I forgot he was seeing her tonight.'

'Shut that front door!' Dad roared.

'Are you coming in?' I asked.

'Well . . .'

'Well, why don't you come in while you're making up your mind whether you're coming in?'

He came into the hall. 'I just came to see if Tim would come out with me for a swift half pint.'

He seemed different: a bit quiet and a bit subdued. A wing of soft, dark hair hung across his forehead.

'Can't she go as well, then?'

'Carol? Not likely. She's a friend of Danielle's.'

'Have you two split up?'

He shook his head. 'She's just gone a bit offish. I thought Tim might help me drown my sorrows.'

'I'll go and ask him if you like . . .'

'No, it's OK,' he said quickly. 'Don't bother him. I'd better be off, anyway.'

'How about a coffee instead?' I heard myself asking.

He raised his eyebrows, then shrugged. 'Why not?'

'You might as well. As you're here,' I said, trying to hide my own surprise that I'd actually asked him. Dealing with boys seemed to get easier as I got older.

We went through into the kitchen and I cleared a pile of tea towels from a chair so he could sit down. I busied myself filling the kettle, getting out the mugs, locating the coffee. Now that he was sitting here with me I didn't quite know what to do with him.

'Who came in?' Vicky said, peering round the door.

I groaned, turned and glowered at her. 'Only Jonno,' I said, 'no one you need concern yourself with.'

She stared from me to him and back again. 'Oh,' she said, and disappeared.

'Those two are *awful*,' I said to Jonno. 'They read things they're not supposed to, listen in to telephone conversations – I even caught them following me the other night, *spying* on me.'

'It's only because they want to be like you,' he said. 'They're just jealous because they're not sixteen and pretty with half a dozen boys after them.'

'Oh, go on!' I said, and it was a good job I was still searching in the cupboard for coffee or he might have seen me go red. 'Don't be daft.'

Jonno stretched and leaned back against the wall. I found the coffee and turned to look at him. 'You don't look all that happy.'

'I'm not.'

'Because . . . because of Danielle?'

He nodded.

'I thought you'd be able to do no wrong now. After buying her that lovely chain, I mean.'

He shrugged. I poured the hot water into the mugs, added milk and put one of them down in front of him. For a while he was so deep in thought I don't think he even knew it was there.

'It started on her birthday really. She got this huge great card from her ex-boyfriend.'

'And did you mind?'

'I did, but I didn't say anything. She keeps bringing it

to my notice, though – every time I go round for her the blasted card is on show.'

'Perhaps she's trying to make you jealous.' I sat down in front of him, sipped at my coffee. I felt very sensible and sophisticated sitting there listening to a boy's problems.

'It's getting beyond a joke – hearing about *him* all the time. He had a car, you see, so every time we go out now she makes a fuss about having to go on the bus.'

'Isn't your motorbike ready?'

He shook his head. 'That'll never be finished. Besides, she wouldn't go on a *bike*.' He noticed the coffee, picked it up and took a mouthful. 'This ex of hers, Gary, she never stops talking about him. I know all the places he used to take her, what he dresses like, what terrific fun he was – he hangs about like an uninvited ghost and I'm just about sick of him!'

'I know how you feel,' I said sympathetically. 'This boy I like, Leo – well, I'm almost going out with him – he's got someone lurking in his background. Tricia, her name is.'

'An old girlfriend?'

I shrugged. 'I don't know. She's a friend of the family or something – but I keep hearing from my friends how *fabulous* looking she is.'

'Some friends!'

I had a sudden thought. 'Maybe we can get the two of them together!'

'Tricia and Gary? It should be a good match seeing as he's Mr Universe and Mastermind rolled into one.'

'Well, then!'

The same thought must have occurred to each of us because we both raised our mugs: 'Tricia and Gary!' we said together, and burst out laughing.

'Hello, hello!' Tim said, coming in and looking at us slyly. 'What's all this, then? My best mate and my kid sister having private chats together in the kitchen, eh? What's going on?'

'Nothing!' I said quickly.

'We're doing a double agony aunt act. Pouring out our troubles,' Jonno said.

'Oh yeah?' Tim turned his attention to me and smiled his best, most wheedling smile. 'How about making coffee for me and Carol while you're chatting, then? I expect Mum and Dad and Rachel would like one, too.'

'What about Vicky and Vanessa?' I asked sarcastically.

He looked at me innocently. 'Do they like coffee?'

'How about *you* making it?'

'Me? I don't know where anything is.'

'Then it's about time you did!'

'All right, all right.' He looked at Jonno. 'See what she's like; proper little spitfire when she's roused. I bet she made *you* a coffee, though.'

'She did, actually.'

Tim nodded. 'See! I told you she fancied you.'

'I do not!' I banged my coffee mug down on the table. 'Honestly! Can't a girl even chat to someone without *you* trying to make something of it?'

'Quite,' Jonno said. 'Besides, she's already going out with someone, aren't you, Mandy?'

'I don't know about that,' I said – and noticed with a shock that Tim was actually looking round for the coffee mugs.

'Second best,' he muttered, looking under the sink and in all the wrong places. 'She might have someone else but he's only second best. It's you she's got her eye on, old mate!'

'Oh, really!' I snatched my coffee mug off the table and stood up. I'd enjoyed chatting to Jonno but Tim was obviously determined to interfere and make me look stupid.

'Ah, you're going to make the coffee after all!'

'No, I'm not, I'm going upstairs!' I gave Jonno an apologetic look; it wasn't *his* fault my family ruined everything. 'Goodnight!' I said to him. 'And the coffee mugs are in the washing-up bowl. Dirty.' I said as a passing shot to Tim.

I went upstairs, where Vicky and Vanessa were getting ready for bed – swinging from the top bunk onto the lower one with great crashings of springs.

'You like Jonno, don't you?' Vicky asked.

I ignored her.

'Do you like him better than your boyfriend?'

'Oh, be quiet!' I sat down on my bed.

'Will they have a fight over you?'

'Who do you like best *really*?'

I stood up again, looking longingly at the cupboard. There was no chance at all of getting in there for some peace and quiet now, though.

'Be quiet and go to bed!' I said fiercely.

'What's up with her?' I heard as I went out onto the

landing. 'Is it her *love* problems?'

I sighed heavily. I couldn't stay in my bedroom, I didn't want to go downstairs. Where could I go?

There was nowhere — so I drank the rest of my coffee standing on the landing. It was cold out there but at least I was on my own. And tomorrow I'd be seeing Leo.

Chapter Seven

He wasn't at school the next day. I didn't find out until lunchtime when Tracey came up and stood next to me in the cold snacks and sandwiches queue.

'I hear lover-boy's got 'flu, then,' she said.

'Who?'

'Don't give me that! You know who I mean; your darling Leo.'

'*Has* he?' I said. 'Is he all right?'

There was a note of alarm in my voice and she looked at me strangely.

'Of course he's all right,' she said. 'He hasn't got malaria or beri-beri or anything, only '*flu*.'

'Sometimes it can be nasty,' I said. I saw him lying, ashen, on one of the pastel settees. I saw him with a white flannel to his head, calling weakly: 'Mandy, Mandy . . .'

The woman behind the counter roared at me to catch up. 'There's four hundred behind you, you know,' she said, 'get a move on!'

I hurriedly took a ham sandwich and a trifle – I don't know why, because I hate ham and the trifles at school are those synthetic ones that taste of dry sawdust. How long would 'flu last? I wondered. He and I were supposed to talk about our date today, too.

'How did you know?' I asked Tracey, going over with her to sit at Laura's table.

'I heard Nigel Potter telling their tutor.'

'I wonder how bad it is?'

'Why are you getting so worried about him?' Laura asked, breaking into the conversation. 'He'll be back in a couple of days. You can live without him for two days, can't you?'

'Of course I can.' I bit into the sandwich and made a face. The ham was more fat than lean.

'Anyway, like I keep saying, it's a waste of time you getting interested in him with Tricia around.'

I almost smiled to myself. Little did they know he'd walked me home and almost kissed me. *And* telephoned me the next day.

'What school does she go to?' Laura asked curiously.

'A private one. I think they do drama and stage work mostly.'

'Lucky devil!'

'She's really talented by all accounts,' Tracey went on. 'Quite sickening, it is. I mean to say, some girls have *everything*.'

'No wonder Leo's taken with her, then,' Laura said.

'It's a wonder half the country aren't taken with her,' I said, stung into speaking. 'The way you talk about her it's a wonder she hasn't got Twentieth Century Fox and Metro Goldwyn Mayer at each other's throats trying to sign her up.'

'Well, well,' Laura said. 'Do I detect the slightest trace of jealousy?'

'Not at all,' I said, fighting down my irritation. 'But I don't know why you have to keep on about how wonderful she is. Anyway, Leo's told me all about her. As a matter of fact she rang while I was at his house on Friday.'

I knew I shouldn't have risen to the bait because I hadn't meant to tell them a thing about Leo and me, but they'd goaded me into it. Anyway, it was only two quite small lies *and* it was a way of letting them know I'd been at his house.

'Well!' Tracey said.

'Doing magazine work, were you?' Laura asked.

'Not only that,' I said cagily. 'He walked me home after, of course.'

'So what about this Tricia?'

'What about her? She's a very good friend of the family.'

'So are you going out with Leo?' Laura asked, her voice rising with a mixture of incredulity and disbelief.

'I didn't say that. I *could* be, though.'

She and Tracey exchanged glances; they clearly thought I was kidding myself.

Leo didn't come back to school on Tuesday or Wednesday – and on the Wednesday afternoon Nigel found me during a free period and pushed a lot of papers at me.

'The completed letters page for the magazine and some reviews,' he said, 'they just need a final looking-over.'

'I think that's everything, then,' I said. 'Leo and I have gone through the rest of the contents.'

He peered at me over his glasses. He's got zappy tinted glasses with navy blue frames but on him they're not trendy. 'Susie Ellis said she'd type everything out for us.'

'Great!' I said. 'What about the printing? Leo did say he'd be talking to the school secretary.'

'In Leo's absence I've spoken to him,' Nigel said solemnly. Nigel's dead serious; I don't think I've ever seen him laughing. 'It can be run off on the new machine, all we've got to do is supply the paper.'

'Is that *all*?' I asked, a bit sarcastically.

He peered sternly at me again. 'It's all taken care of. Susie and I have spoken to the head of upper school and she's going to make sure the paper is paid for out of the school activities fund.'

'Great!'

'Only the first issue, of course,' he said dourly, as if to ensure that I didn't get too happy about it. 'After that we're expected to be self-supporting.'

I refused not to be happy, though. 'So we're nearly ready to roll?' I asked excitedly.

'Nearly. We'll want Leo's final word on the stuff I've just given you, of course.'

'Of course,' I agreed.

'So if you could get it round to him tonight I'll pick it up in the morning. Even if he's in bed at least he'll be able to look at it.'

'Me?' I said, feeling panicky. 'Me go round there?'

'You're co-editor, aren't you?' Nigel pointed out. 'I thought you'd want to.'

'Yes. Of course,' I said hastily. Of course nothing. Nigel didn't know how embarrassing it would be to go round to the house of someone you didn't know if you were going out with or not. Especially if he was in bed.

'Tell him I'll collect it in the morning and then we can pass everything on to Susie.'

'Is there any hurry?' I said. 'He might be back at school tomorrow anyway.'

'I don't reckon he will,' Nigel said. 'And we ought to give Susie as much time as possible to type it – she's only been on the commercial course a term and she's not all that fast.'

'OK,' I said, my heart sinking. I could see I wasn't going to be allowed to get out of it.

'Tell him to read all the letters,' Nigel said, pausing in the doorway. 'I've collected some rather good ones.'

'Right,' I said hollowly.

As it was a free period I went through the letters myself. Because no one had actually written to the magazine yet, of course, Nigel had put a notice up on all the different forms' notice boards asking for 'printable comments' about the school or otherwise.

Most of them were about school. There were the usual grouses from first and second years about school dinners, some moans about the amount of homework we got, and a passionate plea that school uniform be abolished.

There were a few lighter ones: a couple containing jokes about different teachers, one from someone who wanted to start a lonely hearts club – was there anyone out there interested? – and one from someone who asked what all the fuss was about pop stars who were gender benders: didn't everyone realize that things had just come full circle historically, that men had been wearing make-up and wigs two hundred years ago so it was nothing to get excited about.

When I gathered up my things ready to go home the panicky feeling came over me again. I had to go round there that evening; round *there* to the elegant house with the Japanese flower arrangements and the mother in stretch velvets.

A thought struck me: a thought which, if I was truthful, had been hovering about trying to make a landing ever since Monday. OK, so he was ill in bed and we couldn't arrange to see each other, but why hadn't he rung me? He wasn't *so* ill that he couldn't come downstairs, surely – and he must know I'd be wondering what was up.

I arrived home to a madhouse which was slightly more mad than usual; much to my horror, the twins each had a friend to tea. I can never see why they need to have friends in. They've got each other and, to my way of thinking, each other should be enough for anyone.

In the kitchen Mum was up to her elbows in potato

peelings and the air was blue with smoke from the chip pan. 'I'm feeding the youngsters first,' she said above the noise of them chattering and banging their knives and forks on the table.

'What time is our tea, then?'

'About six. When Dad comes in.' She beamed at the twins and their friends. 'Two sittings today, eh? Like a holiday camp!'

I disappeared hastily. Sometimes it seems to me that Mum's being taken advantage of; it's always the twins having friends to tea, hardly ever the other way round. I mean, I *know* when they're out because the house is wonderfully peaceful and I have my room to myself, and it hardly ever happens, believe me. I suppose people think that as Mum's got five children, having one or two extra round for tea doesn't make much difference. I don't like to think of my easy-going little mum being taken for a ride, though, *especially* when it means I have to put up with two extra kids underfoot.

I started going through my wardrobe. Not the green dress again, obviously, because Tim had said I looked like a pea pod in it. But then again Jonno had said I looked like a willow tree. Jonno . . . I wondered how he was getting on with Danielle. OK, I supposed, because he hadn't been round asking Tim to help him drown his sorrows again, so maybe they'd made it up and she'd decided not to keep harping on about that Gary of hers.

It had been funny, really, Jonno sitting down and talking to me the way he had. I was pleased, though, because it showed that he must think I was grown up and worth bothering with. I'd like to tell him about Leo sometime, too. Get a fella's eye view of things.

I went through my wardrobe twice more. I was looking for something fashionable rather than trendy; something expensive, well cut and a bit elegant – and of course there was nothing. In the end I selected a burgundy corduroy skirt and a white jumper. The white jumper was one of Mum's laundering casualties and wasn't nearly as white as when it arrived in the house, but it would have to do.

I fiddled about trying to do something different with my hair and discovered that it was *just* long enough to put up on top of my head in a very high pony tail.

It looked quite good, I thought, turning backwards and forwards in front of the mirror. Rather sophisticated.

I laid out the skirt and jumper on my bed and was just about to go downstairs again when the twins came in with their friends.

'What *have* you done to your hair?' Vanessa asked.

'You look like . . . like a coconut!' Vicky squealed, and they all burst out laughing.

I smiled my most withering smile. 'Of course, I forgot, you know all about fashions in hair styles, don't you? I mean, just look at how good *you* look.'

They stared at me, not knowing whether to risk giggling again or not. I warmed to my theme: 'It's lovely to have such fashion experts in the family to give me advice. You know all about *haute couture*, do you?'

'What's oat cot-ewer?' Vicky asked.

I smiled again, even more witheringly. 'Don't you *know*?'

I was being childish but I'd discovered that that was the only way to get at them – play them at their own game.

I took another glance or two at myself in the mirror as they disappeared into Vicky's bunk hideout – I didn't really look like a coconut, did I? – and then I began to gather all my things together. Every brush and comb, every morsel of make-up, pot of cream, scrap of paper and school book I put into a cardboard box which I then put into my wardrobe and locked the door. Oh, I'd learnt my lesson long ago. Once they'd had friends in and they'd all come down wearing my clothes. They'd paraded up and down in long skirts and enormously baggy tops, making Mum, Dad and Rachel laugh at their efforts to walk on high heels – and making me storm off to the bathroom (I hadn't discovered the toy cupboard then) crying tears of outrage. Another time they'd used my make-up to do each others' faces (most horribly) and once they'd gone right through my school books and come down to report to Mum how many times I'd got lunchtime detentions.

Over the years I'd come to the conclusion that twin younger sisters were the worst deal anyone could have. As well as having my nose put out of joint in the first place when they were born, now I had two of them goading each other to do more and more awful things. One younger sister would be bad enough, but two together presented a united, irresistible force. What one didn't dare do, the other did. Even when they got told off by Mum, which wasn't often, seeing as she passed everything off as 'high spirits', they always had each other to turn to for consolation.

'I'm going downstairs now,' I said fiercely, and the hideout sheet quivered. 'It's no use searching for anything because it's all hidden away in my wardrobe — and if you dare touch anything in my chest of drawers you can be sure I'll know about it!'

Vicky popped her head round the sheet. 'Are you going out with your boyfriend?' she asked, 'Is that why you've got your hair funny?' She turned and obviously addressed the two friends, 'She's got a boyfriend,' she said impressively.

I clenched my fists. 'Just remember what I've told you!' I said warningly.

Downstairs Mum was peeling more potatoes. There were two chip pans at the ready and you could hardly see across the kitchen for smoke. I didn't feel like anything greasy to eat really — and besides, the smell of chips always gets into your hair — but it was easier to eat what was put in front of me rather than have an inquisition from Mum as to why I wasn't hungry.

'Going out, dear?' she said, spearing sausages. 'Your hair looks nice.'

'I don't look like a coconut, do I?' I asked.

'Of course you don't — whatever gave you that idea? Besides, coconuts aren't red-headed, are they?' She looked at me fondly, 'You've got your dad's colouring right enough. You're the only one with exactly his lovely reddy-gold colour.'

'He hasn't got much left now.'

'Ah, but when he was younger he had all the girls after him because of his hair,' Mum said.

'Fancy.' Girls must have changed, then. Boys whose hair was verging on ginger were definitely no-go now.

'I've got to go out after tea,' I said. 'It won't be much longer, will it?'

'I shouldn't think so, dear.' Mum, tutting and disorganized, rolled a sausage into the sink and dropped a coil of potato peeling onto the floor. 'I'll pick that up in a minute,' she muttered.

'I'll do it.' I swooped down and picked it up, then got the plates down. Anything to hurry the meal up a bit. Tim wandered through, picked up a cooked sausage and started nibbling at it.

'What a fancy hairdo!' he said. I looked at him sternly. 'It's all right, I wasn't going to say you looked like a coconut; the twins have already told me I mustn't.'

'It doesn't, does it?' I wailed.

He stood back and studied me, head on one side. 'No, it . . . it looks OK,' he said.

My jaw dropped; 'OK' from Tim was just about the height of praise. 'Well, thanks,' I said.

'But I don't know why you're bothering.'

'What d'you mean?' I asked, puzzled.

'He's not coming round. He's seeing Danielle tonight.'

I heaved a big, irritated sigh. 'Oh, do stop going on about *him*.'

We sat down for tea at last – Rachel said nothing about my hair, just smirked – and then I dashed upstairs to get ready. I had to use the bathroom for changing in, of course, as my bedroom was under invasion, and by the time I'd finished pulling off one jumper and putting on another in that small space, my hair was hanging down in wisps all over. I was scared to take it down completely in case it refused to go back up, so I just had to leave it. To be truthful, I quite liked the wispy look; I thought I looked a bit like one of those Sunday supplement models who're photographed in front of wind machines. Well, just a *tiny* bit!

I set off, all the magazine stuff in my bag, and reminded myself all the way that I was merely going to see the editor of the school magazine, on business. Nigel sent me, I would say if his mother answered the door.

It was beginning to get dark by the time I reached Elstree Crescent. Winter evenings might mean cosy family chats round the fire to some people, but to me they mean the twins never going out after tea and being constantly underfoot and Tim – if it was anything like last year – being allowed to work on his bike in the hall instead of the nasty cold garage. I ask you, have you ever heard of anyone being allowed to bring their motorbike *indoors*?

I reached Leo's house, smoothed my hair, adjusted my jacket collar and walked up the path to his front door. 'Hello, Mrs Mann,' I would say in my best speaking voice, 'Nigel asked me to call . . .'

I rang the bell and the 'Hello Mrs' died on my lips,

because it was answered by a girl about my own age, a girl with hair that was longer and straighter and blonder than Jerry Hall's.

My heart sank. This, obviously, was Tricia.

Chapter Eight

'Hello,' I said weakly.

'Yes?' She looked at me as if she thought I was going to offer to sell her some clothes pegs.

'I . . . er . . . came to see Leo. Is he all right?' She still didn't say anything so I added: 'Nigel from school asked me to come.'

'Oh.' She hesitated for a moment and then called over her shoulder: 'Leo! There's a girl here for you.'

I stood there for a few seconds feeling as awkward as could be and then Leo's head appeared round the sitting-room door.

'Oh, it's Mandy!' he said. 'Come in!'

I went into the hall; behind me I could hear Tricia closing the door and sense her looking me up and down.

'Come and sit down,' Leo said, smiling at me. His face was pale enough for his six freckles to show up and I longed to put my arms round him and give him a get-well hug. 'This is Tricia, by the way. I don't think you two have met, have you?'

We both shook our heads and stared at each other. She had the hair all right – and the bust, come to that – but I didn't think her face was going to set Hollywood alight. She had a horrible expression on it for a start, as if she had a nasty smell under her nose. Maybe that was just because she was looking at me, though.

I could see straight away that she did have one big advantage over me: she was clearly at ease, both in the house and with Leo. She sat herself on one of the settees, shoes off and feet tucked under her, looking as if she was going to make me feel out of it and enjoy doing so.

'Sit down!' Leo urged again, and I sat on the very edge of a satin chair. 'What brings you round, then?'

'I . . . I wanted to see how you were,' I said, 'and then Nigel asked me to get your OK on some magazine stuff. Susie wants to start typing it as soon as she can.'

'Right!' Leo said, and he bumped along his settee to get nearer to me and take the file I was holding.

'How are you, anyway?'

'Not so bad, not so bad.' He flicked through the pages while I looked round the room we were in, seeing things I hadn't had time to notice the previous Friday. The walls were very pale green, with the two or three little shelved alcoves picked out in white. One wall, the small end one, was completely covered in mirrors: round ones, square ones, ones with fine gold frames and one with a border of stained glass.

My gaze came back to Tricia. I smiled at her politely

and then looked away quickly because she didn't smile back.

'All this looks fine,' Leo said, looking up from the papers.

'Nigel said if you look through them tonight he'll collect them tomorrow morning.'

'I'll do that.' He stretched his arms lazily; he was wearing a white shirt in some very soft, thin material. I'd seen him in it before – he'd been wearing it at a party one of the Sixth formers had given just a week into term and it had been then that I'd first noticed him. He'd been dancing at the time and the shirt was quite full so it sort of billowed out in some places and clung to him in others. I thought he looked like Romeo in it.

'I should have rung you,' he said now. 'I've been feeling like death for three days, though. In fact, I've only just got up.'

'But you're feeling better now?'

'Much better.'

'And you're coming back to school tomorrow, then?'

He shook his head. 'I thought I might as well take the rest of the week off.'

'And you *did* say you'd come to the display at college on Friday!' Tricia said, and I felt my stomach knot itself into a tight little lump.

'I haven't forgotten.' Leo looked at me. 'Tricia's at a drama and music college and they've got this show Friday afternoon for parents and people.'

'Leo, you make it sound so *naff*,' Tricia drawled. 'It's actually for agents.'

'Is it like on "Fame"?'

'*God*, no! That's an insult!'

'Apparently it's all a lot more professional than "Fame",' Leo explained.

'We just *shudder* when anyone mentions "Fame"!' Tricia added, shuddering dramatically to show me how. There was another silence, then: 'You're in this magazine lark, too, are you? What do you do, more of the typing?'

'No, some of the features,' I said. I *knew* she was trying to get me niggled. 'I can't type.'

Leo flicked through the magazine pages again. Tricia and I looked anywhere but at each other. I wondered how to go; if I should go. But then maybe if I waited *she*'d go.

I looked down and noticed a white mark, like toothpaste, on my burgundy skirt. Surreptitiously I licked my finger and scratched at the offending patch. Out of the corner of my eye I took in what she was wearing; only jeans, but they looked like designer ones, and with them a pink silk tee-shirt. I sighed inwardly, how did I get myself in the sort of situation where my rival wasn't an ordinary girl at school but a potential *star*; the sort of person who wore designer jeans and silk tee-shirts? It wasn't fair, Leo should have had a government warning on him.

Leo looked up and I felt him study me carefully. 'It's your hair!' he said suddenly. 'I've been wondering what it was about you that was different.'

'Oh yes. I've put it up.'

'Looks super! You look like a ballet dancer.'

I carefully didn't look at Tricia in case she was smirking a Rachel-type smirk. If she hadn't been there I would have laughingly told Leo about Vicky saying I looked like a coconut, but I certainly wasn't going to say it in front of *her*.

She stretched and yawned and my heart jumped, thinking that she was going to get up and go, but she didn't. Maybe it was a hint for *me* to go. I had a sudden urge to let her know that Leo and I were much more than just magazine co-editors. Let *her* feel out-of-it and awkward. I turned to Leo and smiled brightly.

'Sorry about all the row when you phoned me on Sunday,' I said. 'First of all I couldn't get rid of the twins and then I stretched the phone lead across the hall and Dad went and fell over it.'

'I wondered what was going on. Why did you stretch the lead across the hall?'

'To get the phone into the sitting room and away from the twins,' I explained. 'I couldn't hear what you were talking about.'

'You ought to get an extension put in your room,' Tricia said. '*I* went through all that – could never speak to my friends without interruptions – so I asked Dad to get an extra phone.'

'That's an idea,' I said, silently shrieking to myself. *Imagine*! Imagine Dad's face if I asked for my own phone extension! Anyway, it wouldn't be much good because if it was in my bedroom the twins would still be there. It would have to go in my cupboard.

I was just about to say something else about the phone call — not that she was looking the least bit perturbed — when there was the sound of a key in the lock and then Leo's mother called, 'I'm home!'

She came straight into the sitting room. 'How are you, darling? Feeling better?' she said to Leo, then, 'Hello, Trish. Your mother said you were coming over.' She seemed to notice me just as she was going out, 'Oh, it's your friend from school!' she said, making me feel about seven. 'Mary, isn't it?'

'Mandy,' I said.

'Of course. How are you, dear? And is the school going to pieces without my Leo?'

I laughed dutifully.

'I'm parched, I'll go and get the coffee on. Everyone stopping for coffee?'

I nodded; she obviously meant was I stopping because she was looking at me.

She went out and some five or six minutes later came back with a tray bearing milk, sugar and a plate of biscuits. I don't know what Leo, Tricia and I talked about during those five or six minutes but the conversation wasn't easy, I do know that.

'Bring the cups in for me, Trish, will you?' she said, putting the tray on a low table. 'Pink ones, usual cupboard.'

She went out and Tricia followed her. I looked unhappily at Leo. I wanted to go home; actually wanted to go home to the madhouse, that's how awkward I felt. I longed for Leo to say something to me, something to make it all right, something that would bring back that moment on Sunday when he'd talked about kissing me . . .

There wasn't time, though. Within a few seconds his mother came back carrying a glass coffee jug and Tricia followed with cups and saucers.

'She'll obviously tell you later but your mother and I made utter fools of ourselves tonight!' Leo's mother said, putting the coffee down on a pink table mat and addressing Tricia.

'French, wasn't it?' Tricia said. 'Oh Mummy's an absolute duffer at French.'

'So am I, believe me!'

'You couldn't be as bad as Mummy. She can't get the hang of the pronunciation at all – sounds just like your typical Englishwoman abroad!'

'The tutor's an absolute poppet, though. I think we'll stick at it just to see him!'

I smiled – I was doing an awful lot of those tight, polite little smiles – and thought about Mum going to French classes and calling the tutor an 'absolute poppet'.

'She and I fought over who was going to sit next to him at break!' Leo's mother went on, pouring the coffee.

I took the cup she offered and sipped at it delicately, trying to make neat little movements. All I needed now was to make a loud slurping noise or drip it onto the white carpet.

'Did you get the college disco tickets arranged all right?' she asked Tricia. 'Leo was a naughty boy, wasn't he, he didn't ring you in time.'

'Ma!' Leo protested.

'It was all right, I had two already,' Tricia said. 'I just wondered if Leo wanted some more – to make up a party from his school.'

Leo nodded. 'I was thinking of it. I wondered if I could get all our magazine staff along,' he said to me. 'It might have been a laugh.'

'Oh, you should have done,' I lied, thinking that the last place I wanted to go was *her* college disco to watch her swanning about with her friends.

'I got sick instead and it went completely out of my mind. Still, I don't suppose people like Nigel would have wanted to come, anyway.'

'He might have done. Perhaps he's a wow on the dance floor,' I said. It felt like the longest sentence I'd spoken for ages.

'Talking of being a wow on the dance floor,' Tricia said, 'guess who's been picked for the solo in the jazz dance?!'

We all looked at her. Well, we didn't really have to guess, did we?

'Marvellous!' Leo's mother said. 'That's one of the pieces on Friday, is it?'

'Ah-huh,' Tricia murmured smugly.

'Oh, we'll look forward to seeing that, won't we, Leo?' She didn't wait for Leo to say anything, just went on: 'We've got quite a little star in our midst, haven't we?!'

I nodded, feeling that I'd like to jump on the little star and strangle her.

They carried on talking about the show and about

Tricia's talents in excited voices (it sounded exactly like 'Fame' to me) while I got more and more fed up. The knotted feeling in the pit of my stomach still hadn't gone away – and was being joined now by a headache caused by my hair being dragged back.

My coffee finished, I made myself stand up. 'I ought to be off. Thank you very much for the coffee,' I said, and I couldn't help the trace of sarcasm in my voice.

Three pairs of eyes looked at me – and I knew that two of them were assessing my clothes, pricing my shoes and noting that my tights were the cheap sort that went into a fold round the ankles. Leo stood up, too.

'Leo, you're not to dream of going out!' his mother said sharply. 'Not when you've been in bed for three days.'

'All right, all right!' he said. He sounded rather irritated with them, I was pleased to note.

'Goodbye Mrs Mann. Goodbye Tricia, see you!' I said, hoping I never would.

'Bye-ee!' they both cooed.

Leo went with me into the hall and opened the front door. A peal of laughter came from Tricia and I tried to ignore it.

'Thanks for coming round,' he said, 'sorry I haven't phoned you.'

'That's OK. I know what it's like when you've got 'flu.'

'And I'm sorry I can't take you home.'

'It doesn't matter.' His eyes looked very green in the soft light coming from the lamp on the wall, and as I looked into them I suddenly realized that he was going to kiss me.

For a second I wavered; I wanted him to kiss me – oh boy, *did* I want him to – but I wanted it to be an intense, meaningful kiss – not one in which Tricia and his mother were warbling away in the background and putting me off. I backed away from him; he looked surprised.

'I'll see you when you get back to school, then,' I said quickly.

'Sure. Or maybe I'll ring you at the weekend.'

'Leo! There's an awful draught!' his mother called shrilly.

'Oh well, I'd better go!' I slipped past him and out of the door, then practically ran across the road. When I got to the other side I looked back, but he'd gone indoors.

I pulled my jacket round me and walked on, my eyes stinging. I'd never felt so miserable and *small* in my life. I could almost hear his mother and Tricia discussing me as soon as the door shut: 'Who was that person?' Tricia would say, and his mother would wave her hand dismissively, 'No one of any account. Some girl from Leo's school – comes from a very large family and lives on Parkview Estate.'

I quickened my footsteps. I wanted to get home before I started crying properly.

I was running by the time I reached my road – running as if somehow I'd be able to shake off all my anger and humiliation. I let myself in and carried on running upstairs, calling 'I'm back!' to Mum and Dad as I did so and pulling my hair out of its top-knot.

I was about to enter my bedroom, but then I heard the twins talking. It was nine-thirty and they were *still* awake. Frustrated (I couldn't even *cry* in private now) I locked myself in the bathroom, sat on the side of the bath and promptly burst into tears.

I hated them — both of them! It had started off so promisingly, Leo and me, but now . . .

'Mandy! Is that you in there?' Rachel's bossy voice rose above the rattling of the door handle.

'Yes,' I said in a muffled voice.

'Well, are you going to be long? I want to wash out some tights.'

'Can't you do that downstairs?'

'Not in the kitchen sink I can't!'

'Oh, for goodness sake!'

'Mum prepares the vegetables in that sink,' she said in her self-righteous voice. 'It wouldn't be hygienic.'

I reached for a damp flannel and pressed it against my eyes. There was nowhere for me to go: *nowhere*.

'Are you coming out?'

'Have I any *choice*?' I said bitterly. I pulled the door open and, not looking at her, slammed out.

The twins were still talking. I knew they'd notice my red eyes like a shot, so there was nothing for it but to go downstairs.

I got to the bottom step; there was a larger-than-usual amount of going-upstairs clutter waiting there but I slid down onto it. It sounded as if Tim and someone else were in the kitchen; Mum and Dad were in the sitting room – and I really didn't feel I wanted to face anyone.

I could have only been sitting there a moment when I heard: 'See you tomorrow!' then the kitchen door opened and Jonno came out. He saw me and I caught a glimpse of Tim and Carol in the kitchen, then he pulled the door quietly shut behind him.

'What's up with you, Sunshine?'

I turned my face away. 'Does anything have to be up? I'm just sitting on the stairs for a while.'

'You've been crying, though.'

'Full marks for observation,' I said miserably.

'Come on now, what's up?' He sat down next to me, half-sitting on the going-upstairs pile.

'Nothing!'

'You can tell me. I thought we were going into the agony aunt business.'

'It's nothing,' I sniffed. I was sitting upright and away from him, very stiff, when what I really wanted to do was put my head on his shoulder and howl.

'It's that boyfriend of yours, I suppose.'

'I haven't *got* a boyfriend.'

'That almost-boyfriend, then. Has he been upsetting you? What's he done?'

I felt new tears come into my eyes at the sympathy in Jonno's voice. 'He . . . it's not him exactly. It's this Tricia. And his mother. I just wish I *knew*.'

'Wish you knew if you were going out with him?'

'Well, that – and who Tricia is, exactly. She was round there tonight and she somehow sort of fits in there. I want to know if she's just a friend, or his ex, or what.'

'I see,' Jonno said. He got a handkerchief out of his pocket, dabbed at my cheeks. 'Difficult one, that. I think you'll have to come out and ask him. Say it's been on your mind and you want to know.'

I leaned against Jonno just a little: it felt warm and comforting. 'I can't do that. We don't have those sorts of conversations.'

'Well, don't you think you ought to start? I mean . . .'

Tim and Carol came out of the kitchen. 'I thought I could still hear your voice!' Tim said. 'Oh, she's grabbed you on the way out, has she?!'

I hung my head. I couldn't be bothered to say anything and I didn't want Tim to see I'd been crying and tell everyone.

'We're going to watch the film,' Tim said. 'Coming in?'

I shook my head and Jonno said it was all right, he was just off. Carol shot me a sympathetic glance and followed Tim into the sitting room.

'You go,' I said. 'I'll be OK. I'm going upstairs now.'

He put his arm round me and gave me a hug. 'Sure?'

'Sure.'

He turned and winked at me as he went out. I stayed on the stairs for a while longer, feeling lost and miserable, and then I shouted to Mum and Dad that I was going to bed.

I listened carefully outside my door but I couldn't hear anything, so I let myself in and began getting ready for bed, looking forward to getting under the covers and shedding a few quiet tears.

I switched off my bedside light, slid under the duvet and sighed deeply.

'We saw you on the stairs with Jonno!' Vicky chirped up suddenly, making me jump.

'We crept out and saw you!' said Vanessa.

I groaned and rolled over.

'Did he kiss you?'

I picked up one of my pillows, pulled it over my head and down across my ears each side. Even so, I could still hear a little piping voice saying: 'Is he going to be your boyfriend instead of that other one; *is* he?' as I lay miserable and sleepless in the dark.

Chapter Nine

'Another Saturday night with nothing to do,' I said mournfully to Sammy.

'Leo'll be back at school on Monday, though. Maybe he'll ask you out for next weekend.'

'Monday's two days, Saturday's *seven* days — I always seem to be waiting.' We were in her bedroom chatting and I settled myself down into her bean-bag cushion until I got the nearest I can ever get to being comfortable in it, and watched her doing her face. 'I'm always sitting here watching you do yourself up, as well,' I said. 'I reckon I know your face better than my own.'

'In that case,' she said, lowering her eyelashes, 'what do you think of the purple mascara?'

'You can't see it's purple. It looks black to me.'

'Blast! Does it really?'

'All this for Graham! I hope he appreciates it.' I paused, then asked: 'How long have you been going out with him now?'

'Four and a half months,' she said promptly. She reached into a box, brought out a bright pink chiffon scarf and tied it into a little bow on the top of her head.

'Wow!' I said admiringly.

'Wow the scarf or wow Graham?'

'The scarf. It looks really ... really Channel Fourish.'

She turned this way and that, then finally got a hand mirror to check her back view.

'Do you really like Graham, though?' I asked after a moment.

''Course I do.'

'*Really* like him, I mean. Properly.'

'Dunno.' She turned to face me, looking vague. 'He's someone to go out with, isn't he?'

'But do your legs go all weak at the thought of seeing him? Does your stomach turn over when he comes into the room? When you kiss him do you see stars?'

She looked at me in amazement. 'You're mad!'

'I feel like that about Leo, though.'

'I didn't think you'd kissed him yet.'

'I haven't. When I do, though, I'm sure it's going to be fantastic,' I said dreamily. 'Bells ringing, fireworks going off . . .'

'Vicky and Vanessa making squelchy kissing noises behind the door,' she finished.

I groaned, rolling forward on the bean-bag and putting my head on my knees. 'What am I going to do about them?' I wailed. 'Even if he does ask me out soon I've still got *them* lurking in the background waiting to spoil things.'

'Maybe you could divert them. Set them on to Tricia.'

I groaned again. 'D'you think he's going out with Tricia?' I asked for the umpteenth time.

She rolled her eyes under eyelids of indigo. 'I don't know – I keep telling you. I don't know her and I don't even know him.'

'But does it sound as if . . .'

'It honestly doesn't sound to me as if he can be,' she said. 'If he was, he would have died of horror when you went round and she was already there.'

'D'you really think so?'

'Of course I do, I keep telling you. I expect they're just convenience friends – they knock about together when there's nothing better to do. They've probably known each other so long that they're like cousins or something.' She opened her eyes very wide at the mirror and began to apply another coat of mascara. 'And now for God's sake stop going on about him.'

'I'll try,' I promised. I crossed my fingers behind my back, though.

*

Sammy went off to meet Graham and I walked home slowly, wondering what Leo was doing and whether he might ring me as he'd said. Maybe tonight was the night of the college dance though? He was probably there with Tricia — she *said* she'd got two tickets. Maybe he was dancing with her right now; I bet she was one of those show-off dancers who always wanted to be in the centre of a crowd of people clapping them along. Still, if she was like that at least they wouldn't be having lots of cheek-to-cheek slowies together. Maybe she was good at those as well, though . . .

As I said, I dawdled home, hoping that by the time I got in the twins would be in bed — or at least on their way to it — and Rachel would either be out or in her room with one of her funny friends going ga-ga over one of their drippy tapes. If I'd known the real situation, of course, I would have *raced* home, put on spiked shoes and torn through the estate beating all records. Come to that, I wouldn't have gone out in the first place.

The first I knew that something was up, though, was when I reached our front gate and looked up at the house. Vicky and Vanessa were at the sitting-room windows, Vicky kneeling on a table in order to get a better view over the hedge.

'Get down!' I mouthed.

To my surprise, she did. In fact they practically fell over themselves to obey me, disappearing from the window as if a magician had clapped his hands. I'd taken a key with me and I dug into my pockets to find it — but as I did so there was a crash as, fighting and

111

panting, they both flung themselves against the front door and fought to open it.

'For goodness' sake!' I said.

Vicky wrenched the door open. 'It's him!' she shrieked.

'Your boyfriend!'

'Here! Talking to Mummy in the kitchen!'

I felt myself go pale. I wouldn't have thought you *could*, but I actually felt all the blood drain away from my face.

'Leo? Do you mean it's Leo?' I asked, panic rising.

'He's been here about ten minutes. Mummy said you wouldn't be long at Sammy's.'

'Oh God!' I said. 'Oh God. Oh God.'

'Why do you keep saying that?'

'Didn't you want him to come round?'

All this had taken place while I was still on the doorstep. I pushed past them and went into the hall, with them following closely behind me like two brides-maids.

I looked at myself in the hall mirror: I did look pale, ghastly pale and awful. 'Oh God,' I said again. I was beginning to sound boring.

'In the kitchen?' I asked.

Vicky nodded excitedly.

I hung back outside the door: what sort of a state was it in, in there? Maybe . . . a gleam of hope . . . maybe Mum had spring-cleaned the kitchen that very evening. Maybe a miracle had occurred and new kitchen units had materialized, the walls had been papered and there were now sunken spotlights in the ceiling instead of the awful fluorescent strip. Maybe Mum was wearing stretch velvet jeans and pouring Leo a percolated coffee . . .

'Aren't you going in?' Vanessa asked.

'Why are you just standing there looking funny?'

I took a deep breath, pushed open the door and Leo turned and smiled at me, looking (I thought) relieved.

He was sitting on a chair at the table. In front of him were two saucepans, a pile of Sunday supplements, a dead pot plant, three milk bottles and the bread bin.

'Hello!' I said with pretend-brightness, as if I was used to coming in and finding the most wonderful guy in the Sixth with his feet under our table and half a hundredweight of clutter in front of him.

'He wouldn't have a coffee and he wouldn't have tea,' Mum said. 'Maybe you can persuade him.'

I turned my attention to Mum. She had on an apron with what appeared to be brown sauce smeared down the front of it and was wearing fluffy slippers and . . . and I can hardly bear to write this . . . a pair of Dad's grey woolly socks. In the front of her hair was a crocodile clip and she didn't appear to be wearing any make-up.

Feeling sick, I went to stand in front of her. Maybe Leo hadn't noticed the socks yet.

'Will you . . . er . . . have something to drink now?' I asked timidly.

'Well, if you are.'

'Get along with you, twins!' Mum said, frowning

towards the door where Vicky and Vanessa clung hopefully onto the door handle. 'It's only Mandy's boyfriend.'

I nearly dropped the kettle I was filling. Mandy's *boyfriend*! Oh, God!

'Tea or coffee?' I asked, my voice shaking.

'Coffee will be fine, thanks.'

The back door crashed open and Tim came in carrying two loud-speakers which he put on the table.

'Say hello to Mandy's boyfriend!' Mum commanded.

'Hi, mate!' Tim said cheerfully, wiping his nose with the back of his hand.

I shrieked a long, silent shriek. It couldn't get any worse, *it couldn't*. I got out two mugs and put coffee in them automatically.

'Can we have coffee too?' Vanessa asked in a wheedling voice. Instead of disappearing they'd come further into the kitchen.

'No,' I said. I smiled a sickly smile at Leo. 'Are you all better now? Back at school on Monday?'

'What did you have, love?' Mum asked. 'Nothing catching, was it?'

'Just 'flu,' I said firmly. If she started on about Mrs Johnson down the road who'd had 'flu for seven months now, I was going to have to put one of the saucepans over her head.

'I . . . er . . . thought I'd better pop round because I remembered I'm not at school on Monday. I've got three days at a computer factory.'

'Computer factory,' Mum said. 'That's nice.'

'We've got electronic computer games,' Vicky said. They'd edged in so far they were standing by the table and practically on Leo's lap now. I never think they look particularly appetizing but they looked quite revoltingly scruffy right then – both in jeans that were frayed round the ankles and shapeless sweatshirts that might have been white once.

'Vicky's got Donkey Kong and I've got Run Rabbit Run,' Vanessa volunteered.

'Leo's not interested in your computer games,' I said, trying to sound gentle and pleasant yet giving them a hard, menacing 'go away' look.

Tim bulldozed his way to the sink, where he turned on the taps full blast and began washing his hands, sending water all over the pile of plates that were balanced, drying, on the side. 'Not too much sugar in mine,' he said. 'Carol says I need to cut down.'

'I haven't made you one.' I looked at Leo and tried to smile. 'Shall we go in the sitting room?' I asked him. 'It must be your bedtime,' I said to the twins.

I carried our coffees through. 'What a surprise!' I said to Leo in the hall, ushering him past the pile of pants and vests destined for upstairs which were waiting on the bottom step. 'If I'd known you were coming I wouldn't have gone round to Sammy's.'

'I thought I'd better,' he said, 'you might have wondered where I was on Monday.'

I pushed open the sitting-room door and gave a whimper of horror. Mum had obviously been ironing because the room was hung about with Dad's and Tim's shirts – fifteen or so of them hung all about the room like flags.

In the middle of all these Dad sat watching TV and Rachel with her headphones clamped to her head was grimly listening to Barry.

'Looks like Christmas,' Leo said, nodding at the shirts.

Feeling slightly hysterical, I rushed round the room collecting them up. It was lovely of him to have thought of me and come round – but I was beginning to wish with all my heart that he'd suddenly remember a pressing appointment and go home. Oh, if I'd only known he was coming I could have arranged things. Made it all different.

'Out of the way!' Dad said, craning his neck to see round me to the television. I stopped with an armful of shirts: 'Dad, this is Leo,' I said.

Dad nodded absently.

'We've met,' Leo said, speaking quietly so as not to interrupt Dad's television. 'He answered the door to me.'

I looked at Rachel. She was looking at the wall, a soppy half-smile on her face. 'Won't you sit down?' I said to Leo wildly.

I ran into the kitchen, pushed the shirts into Mum's arms and ran back again before she could say anything. When I went back in the sitting room Leo was on the edge of a chair running a finger round the inside of his collar and looking desperately uncomfortable.

I pulled one of the straight-backed chairs nearer to

116

him and we sat there sipping our coffee in silence for what seemed like ages. I couldn't think of a thing to say; I should have been able to drum up a comment or two on the magazine but my mind had gone all fuzzy round the edges. Outside I could hear the twins being persuaded to go to bed and Vicky's whining demand that she be allowed to have 'one more look' at Mandy's boyfriend.

'You'll be back at school on Thursday, then?' I asked, to try and cover the whine.

'Yes,' he said. 'Thursday.'

There was another long silence. I could see Rachel looking sideways at us; the headphones were squashing her hair and making her look even frumpier.

'Er . . . was the show good yesterday?' Not that I really wanted to know.

'The show? Oh, at Tricia's college. Yes, it was OK.'

'Only OK?' I asked innocently.

'Oh, all that tap dancing and prancing about on stage isn't really my sort of thing. They're all on ego trips if you ask me.'

'Really?' Especially *her*.

'They like me to go, of course. I have to show willing.'

I swallowed nervously; there was something I just had to ask. 'Is . . . er . . . Tricia your cousin or anything?'

'Trish?' He laughed and Dad shot forward in his seat in order to turn up the sound on the TV. 'No, she's not my cousin; we've just been brought up together, that's all.'

'Oh.'

'Pushed out in our prams and all that.'

I smiled politely; I still didn't really *know*. The film Dad was watching finished and the music blared out for a television quiz game. Dad stood up and switched off the set. 'I'm not having *this* lot of rubbish on,' he said to no one in particular. 'Complete waste of licence money. *Complete* waste.' And he picked up the local evening paper and disappeared behind it.

I looked from Leo to Dad and back again. Was I supposed to include Dad in the conversation now (what conversation?) or just ignore him? Such an occasion had never really arisen before. I'd had boys round, boys that I'd been out with and that Dad knew from the estate, but never a boyfriend as such. It was all different; there were so many difficulties now.

After a minute Tim came in, singing, and turned the television on again. Talk about a three-ring circus.

I looked at Leo despairingly. How were we *ever* going to get to know each other? More important, however was he going to get round to kissing me?

Why didn't he ask me out? Why didn't he ask me to go to the cinema or something with him tomorrow? If I didn't see him then, I wouldn't see him until Thursday.

The presenter on the quiz show made a joke; the audience shrieked with laugher – loud laughter.

'Can't you turn it down?' I said to Tim. How come Dad didn't say anything?

'These shows have got to be watched loud!' Tim said. 'It's all part of the fun.'

Mum came in. She hadn't removed the socks and

they seemed more glaringly obvious, more woolly. 'What do you know?!' she said. 'Next week's our silver wedding!'

'Don't remind me, you'll make me feel old,' Dad said, still behind his paper.

Rachel seemed to come back to reality and lifted an earphone. 'What's that?' she asked.

'Our silver wedding, dear. Twenty-five years wed.'

'Why didn't you say so before?' Rachel asked above the quiz show. 'Are you going to have a party or something?'

'A bit of a knees-up, certainly,' Mum said. 'Any excuse, eh?'

I was hardly taking in what she was saying, just hoping she'd say it quietly then pick up her grey woolly feet and go.

'The family, of course – Gran and the aunts and uncles,' Mum said. 'And friends.' She looked at Leo, 'Boyfriends included!'

'Mum! Leo won't want . . .'

'Of course he will! Next weekend, love, all right?'

'I'll certainly try, Mrs Rossiter,' Leo said politely.

I stood up. I couldn't stand it any more, really could *not* stand it. 'Shall I walk up as far as the Green with you?' I asked Leo. 'I . . . er . . . just fancy a breath of fresh air.'

'Oh. If you like,' he said, looking startled.

I got him out of that house in seconds; if the place had been on fire we couldn't have been quicker.

'It's certainly busy at your house,' he remarked as we were walking down the road.

'Is that what you call it?' I said darkly. 'It's awful –
and it's like that all the time. I can't wait until I'm old
enough to leave home.'

'It's not that bad, is it? Not bad enough to leave
home for?'

'It *is*! Sometimes I just have to get away from them
all.' I glanced at him, wondering whether to tell. I
wanted him to know I liked things to be quiet and
peaceful, though, that I wasn't like *them*. 'There's a
place I go where no one can find me.'

'A shed at the bottom of the garden?'

'No. A cupboard.'

He burst out laughing. 'You're not serious!'

'I am.'

'What, a broom cupboard or something? Or do you
go into the larder?'

'Not a broom cupboard and not a larder.' I hesitated, feeling silly and almost wishing I hadn't said
anything. 'It's just a cupboard in my room. It goes back
a long way and there's this dolls' house in front so no
one knows I'm there.'

He shook his head, laughing still. 'In the cupboard,
that's a good one!'

We walked on and reached the Green. I stopped
walking.

'You don't have to walk back with me,' I said. 'I can
practically see my house from here.'

'I'd better . . .'

'No, really!' I insisted. 'We'll be going backwards
and forwards all night like yo-yo's.' And I didn't want

him near the house again – just in case something else embarrassing occurred.

'What I was going to say was, I'd better kiss you here, then,' he said, and before I knew what was happening and could compose myself with lips neatly puckered and eyes shut he had his arms round me and it was all happening.

The kiss was fine, but it was over too quickly. Before I'd had time to wonder if I could hear bells ringing or anything, a dog had run past us barking and we'd broken apart.

'Goodnight, then!' He sounded remarkably bright and cheerful; I felt a bit wobbly.

'See you in the week,' I said, thinking that there was obviously not going to be a Sunday cinema outing.

'Yes. See you!'

He stood by the Green watching me; I stopped every now and then to wave to him.

When I got in I went straight up to my room. The twins, thank God, were asleep.

I lay there not knowing whether to laugh or cry and going over every minute he'd been in the house and all the embarrassing things that had happened. Wondering, too, what *other* cringe-making incidents had occurred before I'd got in.

I sighed . . . well, if he hadn't asked me out at least he'd kissed me. I'd have to make do with that for the time being . . .

Chapter Ten

'If you say anything – anything at all, I'll murder you!' I said to the twins fiercely.

'Amanda!' Mum said, 'that's a bit much.'

'Can't we even say hello to him?' Vicky asked plaintively.

'What if he says hello to us first?' said Vanessa.

I sighed. 'All right, you can say hello – but you're not to ask anything. You're not to ask if he's my boyfriend or if . . .'

'Can we ask if he's going to marry you and if Vanessa and I will be bridesmaids?' Vicky asked innocently.

I gave a scream.

'It's all right, she's only joking,' Mum said. 'You must know she's only joking.'

I gave a worried sigh and turned to Mum. 'Now, let me look at you,' I said. Leo was coming to the house again – only to call for me – but I was determined that everything was going to be perfect. It was the Friday before Mum and Dad's 'do' as they called it, so the house was actually fairly tidy and free of mess – it was just the people who lived there I was worried about.

'I said to put some lipstick on,' I said to Mum.

'I would have done, dear, but I couldn't find any.'

I rummaged in the kitchen drawer Mum calls her 'bits and pieces drawer'. I don't really know why she calls it that, because *every* drawer in the house is crammed with bits and pieces.

'Here's one,' I said. 'Quickly, put some on.'

'Is it really going to make that much difference?'

'It is to me.' I studied what she was wearing: a blue and white dress – 'Mum! Get that apron off!' – ordinary colour tights and white sandals. 'Haven't you got any other shoes?' I fretted.

'Not to wear round the house. I've got slippers.'

'No!'

'He's not going to notice what I'm wearing on my feet.'

'He *might*.'

Mum turned round and round slowly in the middle of the kitchen. 'Will I do, dear?' she asked. She winked at the twins. 'Anyone would think I was going in for a Miss World contest instead of it just being Mandy's boyfriend coming round.'

'He's not my boyfriend!' I wailed. 'Not properly. You mustn't keep calling him that in case it turns out he isn't.'

'In my day if a young man came to call for a girl and they went out walking then he was her boyfriend,' Mum said firmly.

'Well, it's different now. I might be but then I might not be.'

I cast a worried glance at the twins. 'Now, go and sit in the other room quietly and don't touch anything and don't get dirty. Just sit there with your hands neatly folded and don't move and don't speak.'

They began giggling. I looked at Mum for help.

'They'll be all right,' she said, giving them a push out of the door. 'Goodness, what a worrier you are.'

123

'It's just it was so awful last time,' I said, 'I really want everything to be OK. I want him to see us at our best.'

'Rachel and her friend are already in the sitting room,' Mum said.

'I *know*! I've begged and pleaded with her for them to go upstairs and do whatever they're doing but she won't. Will you ask?'

'Look, dear,' Mum said, 'you aren't going to be here two minutes, are you? I don't mind putting on my best dress if it makes you happy but I don't really see why everyone else should have their lives disrupted just because of him. If he's going out with you then he'll have to fit in with us.'

'He's *not* going out with me,' I said. 'I keep telling you that.'

'All I'm saying is that in the end he'll have to take us as he finds us – and if he doesn't like it then he's obviously not the one for you, is he?'

'Oh, Mum, do you *have* to go into all that now?' I wailed.

There was a knock at the door and I jumped. 'That's him! Now, I'll nip up the stairs and you show him into the sitting room and in a minute I'll come down all nicely and calmly.'

I dashed out and up the stairs leaving Mum muttering: 'I never saw so much fuss made about anyone in my life' on her way to open the door.

Biting my nails and keeping out of sight at the top of the stairs, I heard Mum opening the door and doing me proud down below:

'Oh, hello, Leo. Mandy won't be a moment,' she said. 'Come in, won't you?' and then I heard the sitting-room door opening and closing.

I took a deep breath, counted to ten, then let out the breath slowly, feeling as tight inside as an overwound clock. I was desperate for everything to be all right so that he'd ask me out properly. Tonight – well, it was just another meeting about the magazine, really. We were going round to Nigel's house to talk to him and Sue and Chris about how we were going to distribute the magazine and what we were going to charge for it. It wasn't what I'd call a real date, but if everything went well, if my family didn't scare him off, then maybe he *would* ask me out.

I walked sedately down the stairs and pushed open the sitting-room door. Leo was standing in the bay window talking to Mum and the twins were sitting on their hands on the floor, staring from Mum to Leo and back again as if it was a game of tennis they were watching. In the back of the room Rachel and her friend were sitting silent and awe-struck, listening to some drivel coming from the record player – coming *quietly*, I'm pleased to say.

'Hello!' I said to Leo. 'Sorry I wasn't quite ready.'

'That's OK,' he said, smiling at me. 'I was just . . . er . . . telling your mother that I was sorry but I wouldn't be able to make the party tomorrow.'

'Oh,' I said. I hadn't mentioned the party to him since Mum had (I'd hardly seen him, anyway), thinking that I'd just leave it up to him to decide whether he wanted to come or not. He'd obviously decided he wouldn't be able to stand it.

'It's Tricia's college disco tomorrow,' he said to me. 'I didn't realize they were on the same day.'

'Perhaps you can come on later,' Mum said. 'What time does your disco finish?'

'Well . . . about eleven, I should think.'

'Mum, I don't suppose he . . .'

'Oh, we'll be here rocking and rolling until the small hours!' Mum said, making me squirm with embarrassment. 'Once you get our family together they never want to go home. You come on later!'

'I'll certainly try, Mrs Rossiter,' Leo said.

I began to edge towards the door. Mum had said quite enough – and it seemed to me that the twins were like two small unexploded bombs; at any minute they might come out with something *awful*.

'Mandy, can Vanessa and I use your new bubble bath while you're out?' Vicky asked as I got to the door.

'No,' I said.

'Oh, *please*! You said if we were good you'd give us something . . .'

'I never did!'

'But we have been good and . . .' the voice began to go into its usual high whine and I interrupted hastily with: 'All right, all right, you can have a tiny bit of it.'

'Oh, thanks, Mandy!' they both gushed.

I opened the door. 'See you later!' I said to Mum.

'Yes, dear. And we'll see you tomorrow!' she said to Leo.

We closed the front door behind us and slowly, very

slowly, as we walked down the road I began to unwind. A thought occurred to me: if it was always going to be like this, was it really and truly *worth* it?

'Your sisters . . .' Leo said thoughtfully.

'Horrible, aren't they?' I said bleakly. 'Little beasts.'

'No, I wasn't going to say that. What I was going to ask was, is there anything wrong with them?'

I looked at him. 'What d'you mean?'

'Well, they keep jogging their heads up and down.'

I laughed nervously. 'Oh, *that*. That's because they're both growing their fringes out. They sort of flick their hair back to get it out of their eyes – I don't think they even know they're doing it.'

'Oh,' he said, 'How strange. I thought it was some sort of nervous twitch.'

'Look, don't feel you have to come tomorrow,' I said to Leo awkwardly. The evening had passed uneventfully and a bit boringly and we were outside my front door again where I was waiting with bated breath for his goodnight kiss.

'Well, I'd like to,' he said, 'it might be a bit difficult, though. I said the disco finishes at eleven but I think it's more likely to be nearer midnight, and by the time I've got Trish home and everything . . .'

'That's all right!' I said hastily, just in case he'd been about to say he'd bring her with him. 'Ours will probably finish around that time anyway. Mum always exaggerates.'

'So, if I don't see you then, I'll see you on Monday.' He sounded as if he was relieved to have got out of it.

127

Still, who could blame him for that . . . rocking and rolling till the small hours – Oh, God!

'Hope you enjoy yourself tomorrow,' I said a bit stiffly. Still no date; wasn't he *ever* going to ask me out?

'The discos there are usually quite good.' He put a hand on my shoulder, 'Next time we'll have to make up a party, eh?'

'Lovely,' I said brightly. I waited, tensing slightly, for the kiss. I had the feeling that every curtain at every window in the house was twitching, that six pairs of eyes were watching us.

'Hey!' There was a shout from further down the road and then running footsteps.

'Just wanted to catch you before you went in!' Tim said, pounding up unaware and probably uncaring that he'd just ruined my big love scene.

'What for?' I asked shortly.

'Hello, mate!' Tim said to Leo. 'Oh, just about the party. Carol's made a cake, see, as a surprise for Mum and Dad. I just wondered if you knew anywhere we could hide it until the evening.'

'I don't know. I'll try and think,' I said, my mind more occupied with a kiss than a cake.

'Nice one it is, a big two and a five. You coming, are you?' he asked Leo.

Leo looked regretful. 'Not sure. Might get there for the last hour or so.'

Tim slapped him on the arm. 'In that case we'll save Auntie Vi for you! How about that, eh, Mandy?'

'Yes,' I said, wishing he'd go in.

'Auntie Vi in her long pink knickers!'

I felt myself going red. 'Do you *have* to?'

'I tell you, if you haven't seen the line-up of my aunts doing the hokey-cokey then you haven't lived!'

I smiled a tight, icy smile at Tim, hoping he would interpret it correctly and go in. He seemed quite relaxed, though, leaning on the fence as if he had nothing better to do than hang about and disrupt my love life.

'Get the present all right, did you?'

'Rachel got it,' I said briefly. We'd bought Mum and Dad a silver (well, silverish) clock between us all.

'I wasn't sure about the clock, mind. I fancied buying a silver vase myself.'

'Well, I suppose I ought to be off,' Leo said pointedly.

I looked at him in desperation. If only he'd stay a bit longer, just until we'd got rid of Tim . . .

However, he walked away and unlatched the gate. 'Might see you tomorrow. Have a good time!'

'You, too,' I said insincerely. 'Goodnight!'

Tim looked at me enquiringly as Leo walked off down the road.

'Didn't interrupt anything, did I?'

I turned on him. 'Of course you did, you pig!' I said. 'I hate you! You've ruined my life and I hate you all!'

'Well, what did *I* do?' I heard Tim asking in an injured tone as I slammed off upstairs.

Chapter Eleven

I was in my cupboard. It was ridiculous; I would have laughed if I hadn't felt so fed up. There I was, stuck in a cupboard wearing my best dress, while in the room below a couple of dozen assorted wrinklies were yelling: 'Knees up Mother Brown' and kicking their elastic-stockinged legs in the air.

I wasn't alone in my cupboard, either: next to me was the cake. I'd volunteered to hide it away where no one could find it and then I'd felt so cheesed-off that I'd decided to come up and join it.

Oh, I knew Mum and Dad and the others were having the time of their lives – but I kept thinking of Leo and Tricia at the college disco; of them dancing together, her long blonde hair falling onto his shoulder.

I put my head on my knees . . . me and Leo, well it just wasn't working out like I'd hoped. Sometimes it seemed to me that the only reason my stomach was turning over and my legs going weak was because I was so nervous all the time in case something embarrassing was about to happen. It didn't make any difference whether we were at my house or his house, both places were potential disaster areas as far as I was concerned.

Tim banged the bedroom door open and I stiffened and held my breath. 'Have you seen Mandy?' I heard him call to someone in the hall. 'We want the cake downstairs now.'

He went along looking in all the bedrooms and then

I heard him going downstairs again.

I sighed; I'd obviously have to come out. Crouching, I managed to pick up the cake and lift it over the dolls' house — and had just got it and myself safely out when Vanessa came in. 'Tim's looking everywhere for you. Where have you been?'

'I was just getting the cake.'

'Was it in here? Where did you hide it?'

'I'm not telling you,' I said, smoothing down my dress.

'Was it in a secret place? I'll find it.'

'That's what *you* think,' I said, checking out of the corner of my eye that the cupboard door was shut. All I needed was for them to discover my little secret place.

'Hurry up! We're waiting,' she said impatiently.

I picked up the silver and white cakeboard in my arms and carefully walked down the stairs.

'Here she is!' Tim said as I went into the sitting room, and someone lifted the arm off the record player and everyone 'Oohed' at the cake.

'Well, what a lovely surprise!' Mum enthused, clapping her hands, though I was fairly sure she'd seen it going up the stairs when it arrived.

Everyone gathered round and sung 'For they are jolly good fellows' and then the record came on again ('Forty Sing-along Party Favourites') and general mayhem broke out.

Auntie Vi grabbed me. 'Haven't seen you dancing yet, girl!' she said. 'Come and let your hair down a bit.'

'I've got to go and help in the kitchen,' I said.

'Now, there's nothing to do there!' she said. 'You're

just making excuses!' She waggled her head. 'Let's put the birdie song on, shall we?'

'I don't know how to do it,' I said, backing away. I wasn't going to do the dratted birdie song, not for *anyone*.

Auntie Vi wriggled awkwardly from side to side, making little flapping movements with her hands. 'It's easy, I'll show you!' She wriggled down further, until she was almost sitting on her heels and four inches of pink knicker-leg were showing.

'I'll be back in a minute!' I said, almost running out of the door.

Auntie Chris and Uncle Dave were in the kitchen arguing over the cutting of the cake. Most of the aunties had brought along big plastic boxes full of food: sausage rolls and flans and vol-au-vents, and I started to put these out on plates.

'You go off and enjoy yourself!' Auntie Chris said. 'I can manage this.'

'That's right, off you go and have a dance!' Uncle Dave said jovially.

'No, it's OK.'

'No boyfriend here tonight, then?' Auntie Chris asked.

'He might come later,' I said briefly. Pigs might fly.

I finished putting the food out and there was nothing else for it but to go back into the sitting room – though there was hardly enough room for me.

I squashed myself into the bay window and looked down the road. *Would* he come later? I glanced round the room: did I even want him to come? Suppose

Auntie Vi grabbed him and wanted him to do the birdie song? Suppose Uncle Jack got hold of him and started telling him dirty jokes? There was just no end to the awful things that could happen in this house tonight.

I pressed my face against the cold window pane. Would he come, or wouldn't he? If he did it meant that he liked me and he wasn't bothered what my family were like, but if he didn't . . .

'Aye, aye con*ga*!' Auntie Elly yelled in my ear, and she plucked me out of the window and I found myself being thrust along on the front of a conga line.

Round and round the sitting room she pushed me, out of the door and into the hall. 'Out the front door!' she urged. 'Aye, aye, con*ga*!'

'No . . . no, I can't!' I said. It would be just my luck to meet someone I knew while I was making a fool of myself out there.

I wriggled out of her grasp and ran down the hall. The rest of the line went past me, up the path and down the road, with Vicky and Vanessa bringing up the rear.

Along the hall shelf were Mum and Dad's presents: a silver tray, the clock we'd given them, a toast rack, two vases and some other fairly awful bits and pieces.

'Lovely, aren't they?' Mrs Smith-down-the-road said, coming up behind me. 'And it's so nice to have souvenirs of the day.'

'Lovely,' I lied.

'You're lucky to be part of such a big, happy family, you know,' Mrs Smith went on in a sickly sentimental voice. 'Twenty-five years happily married – there's not so many couples can say that.'

'No,' I said. I looked at her suspiciously; she seemed to be about to burst into tears at any moment.

'And five lovely healthy children! I remember when . . .' she started.

'I must go and check on the food!' I said hastily, backing into the kitchen.

In the corner of the kitchen sat Gran, asleep with her head resting on the wall and her mouth open. My cousins Tina and Louise, about the same age as the twins, were balancing a tray on which were placed about thirty pieces of cake.

'I'll take it in!'

'*I* will. My mum said I could!'

The tray jerked backwards and forwards between them. Outside in the hall the conga line had arrived back and it sounded as if they'd fallen over each other.

I shuffled some plates around that didn't need shuffling and wondered what the chances were of getting back into my cupboard.

'Mandy!' Vicky called. She pushed past Tina and Louise. 'Your boyfriend's here,' she announced importantly.

'My . . . my boyfriend?' I asked in a strangled voice. 'Leo, you mean? Oh, please, *please* not . . .

'Not that one,' she giggled. 'You said we weren't allowed to call that one your boyfriend.'

'She means it's Jonno,' Vanessa said.

A wave of relief washed over me; I really didn't feel up to coping with Leo at this party.

'You are *stupid*!' I said to the twins automatically.

Jonno came through into the kitchen running his hands through his hair. 'Chaos, isn't it?' he said, grinning widely, 'and where are the happy couple?'

I shook my head. 'They could be anywhere.'

'Your mum said I had to be sure to come, so I'd better let her know I have.'

'She could be out on another conga line,' I said, 'or she could be in the other room kicking up her legs and showing her knickers.'

'Like that, is it?'

'You should see my Auntie Vi,' I said. 'Talk about *embarrassing*.'

We squeezed to one side to let two uncles out and someone else in.

'Leo here?' Jonno asked, and I shook my head. 'He had to go somewhere else. A disco with Tricia,' I added bitterly.

The music from the sitting room suddenly went louder. 'Did you bring Danielle?' I shouted above it.

'No chance!'

'I don't blame you not bringing her here. I think I'd rather spend an evening at . . . at a pig market!' I said.

'No, I didn't mean it like *that*.' He suddenly noticed Gran in the corner and grinned. 'She's enjoying herself.'

'I think she's had too much punch.'

'No, I . . . didn't Tim tell you I'd broken up with Danielle?'

I shook my head. 'Tim doesn't tell me things like that.'

'Well, we've finished.' He shrugged. 'She went back

to Gary the wonder boy.'

'Oh.' Uncle Fred pushed past us to get to the fridge for beer. 'Were you very . . .' it seemed wrong to say 'upset' to a boy '. . . very cut-up about it?'

'Not really.' He looked down at his hands, 'I suppose I was expecting it all along. She went on about him enough.' He made a face. 'Anyway, what about you and Leo? And that other girl?'

It was my turn to shrug. 'I don't know. I still don't know.'

He put his arm round my shoulder in a hug. 'Oh, come on, why are we talking about them in the middle of your mum and dad's party? Let's go and have a dance!'

'What, to Viva España?'

'Who cares? No one will know. If you don't tell anyone, I won't!' Laughing, he pushed me across the hall and into the sitting room.

Half an hour later – well, I wouldn't go so far as to say I was enjoying myself, but I wasn't far off it. Jonno joined in everything, flirting with my aunties and flinging them around like they were sixteen – and they loved every minute of it.

'Your young man?' Auntie Vi said to me during a pause.

'No – Tim's best friend,' I said. 'You must have seen him before.'

'If I were thirty years younger I could make a fool of myself over him,' she said, hitching up her bra strap. 'He's the best-looking chap here. I could eat him up for breakfast!'

I giggled, watching him twirling round pretending to

waltz with Auntie Chris. He fitted in well, I'd say that for him. Imagine Leo twirling an auntie around the floor. And he was nice-looking, all right . . .

Someone sent me into the kitchen to get more drinks and I found Mum in there dabbing her eyes.

'Well, I'm glad you've told me tonight, love,' she was saying to Rachel. 'It's deadened the shock a bit.'

'What shock?' I asked, forgetting what I'd come for. Don't say she was planning to run away with Barry Manilow.

'Rachel wants to get a flat,' Mum said. 'Dad says I'm not to stand in her way but I don't know, to me she's still my baby.'

'Mum!' I protested.

'It's not really a flat,' Rachel said. 'More a large bed-sit. A girl at work's flat-mate is moving out and she's asked me to go in with her.'

'I don't know,' Mum said. 'Two young girls on their own . . .'

'I'm almost twenty-one, Mother!'

'I'll have to think about it. I never thought you'd want to leave home – not any of you. It's not because I stopped you redecorating your room last year, is it?'

'Of course it's not. Everyone leaves home in the end, don't they?'

My mind suddenly went into over-drive. Here I was just standing listening and I hadn't twigged that – oh joy! oh bliss! – if Rachel left home I would be able to have her room!

My heart started beating very fast. I tried to speak calmly, though. 'I think it's a good idea, Mum,' I said.

137

'Leaving home – well, it teaches you how to be independent, doesn't it? You learn the value of . . . of money and all that.'

'Exactly,' Rachel said. She looked at me suspiciously, no doubt wondering why I was actually supporting her. 'I'll never learn to run a house otherwise, will I?'

'That's true, Mum,' I said earnestly. 'And Rachel can always come back at weekends, can't she?' She'll have to go in with the twins if she does, I could have added.

'I suppose so.'

'What's this, what's this? A little bird wants to fly the nest, does it?' Uncle Fred said, butting in.

Mum nodded.

'It taught our Anna a lot, that did,' he said. 'We've never regretted letting her go.'

'There,' I said to Mum. 'That proves it, doesn't it?' I turned to Rachel, 'When were you thinking of going?'

'Not before the end of the month.'

'Oh, ages, yet. Plenty of time for you to get used to the idea, Mum.'

In my mind's eye I saw it: my little room, my *own*. I'd paint one wall red, have it covered in posters. I'd put my record player under the window, make a new duvet cover, buy a new lampshade. I'd have a lock on the door and keep the twins out for ever and ever.

I stared at Rachel blissfully. She was wearing a particularly awful nylon dress with a row of plastic beads but I was even willing to forgive her *that*. 'I'll help you move,' I said.

'I'm not going yet!' she retaliated.

'Oh, well, whenever you are. You can have that wooden box Dad made me to keep all your LPs in.'

She looked at me in amazement and then light dawned. 'I know! You're after my room, aren't you?'

'Your room!' I said, as if it had only just occurred to me. 'Of course, I'll be able to move into it, won't I?'

She looked at me with tight lips. She couldn't say anything, though.

'Oh, I suppose I'll get used to it,' Mum said, sighing, and was then whisked away by Dad into the sitting room to dance.

I felt like dancing after her but I just smiled sweetly at Rachel. 'I'll help you talk Mum round,' I said. Oh, you bet I would!

I went back into the sitting room and found Jonno. 'The most *wonderful* thing!' I said, grabbing him between aunties. 'Rachel's leaving home and I can have her room!'

'Is that good?'

'That's fantastic! The best thing that's ever happened to me!'

He held me at arm's length. 'Really? Better than . . . better than Leo?'

'Leo hasn't happened,' I said. 'I thought he was going to but then he didn't.'

Tim and Carol danced past. 'Put him down, you don't know where he's been!' Tim said to me, and I stuck my tongue out at him.

'So it's good news, eh?'

'Really, really good! You don't know what it's been like; I've always had to share with the twins and it's

139

been *awful*!' I gabbled. 'Do you know . . .' I lowered my voice, ' . . . do you know I've been reduced to getting into a cupboard to get away from everything!'

'A cupboard!'

'Honestly. Don't laugh – it was the only place I could be on my own.'

He shook his head. 'I wasn't going to laugh. I've got a place like that as well.'

'A cupboard?' I asked incredulously.

'Not a cupboard! At the top of our block of flats is a fire door and if you push it open you can get out onto a little area of the roof.' He hesitated and I realized that we somehow had our arms loosely round each other – as if we were dancing, but without moving. 'I go up there sometimes when I want to be on my own. It's great – like being in another world. At night you can look down on the town and it's just a big mass of lights, and when you look up all you can see is stars.'

'It sounds lovely. Better than a cupboard.'

'I'll take you up there sometime.'

'Did . . . did Danielle like it up there?'

'Don't be daft, I couldn't have shown it to her – I never even told her about it. She'd have turned her nose up at it; all she'd have seen was the rubbish on the floor.'

I thought of Leo laughing about my cupboard; he hadn't really understood at all. 'I know what you mean,' I said.

'There're only *certain* people you can tell about things like that.' He paused, 'Danielle and I – well, I never really thought we were right for each other.' His

140

fingers pressed my shoulder, we looked into each other's eyes and I knew exactly what he meant: that *we* were right for each other.

He leaned forward, 'I suppose you couldn't show me your cupboard?' he whispered in my ear.

I burst out laughing. 'We can't! I could . . . we could go for a walk, though. You could take me up on your roof.'

'What are we waiting for?' he said.

I went into the hall for my coat. 'Just going out for a breath of air,' I said, passing Dad.

'Who with?' said Vanessa. The twins were both on the stairs; I hadn't noticed them.

'With Jonno, if you must know.'

They nudged each other. 'Aren't you going out with Leo any more?' Vicky asked.

'None of your business. Who said I was going out with him in the first place?' I wriggled into my coat and looked into the sitting room to try and catch Jonno's eye.

'Well, is Jonno going to be your boyfriend now?' Vicky persisted.

My eyes locked with Jonno's and we smiled at each other as he made his way across the room towards me. How long had I liked him? Why hadn't I realized it before? It was all so *obvious* now I knew.

'*Is* he?' Vanessa urged. 'Tell us.'

'Well, yes,' I said thoughtfully. 'I think perhaps he is . . .'

Mary Hooper
Happy Ever After 85p

Marcy is a romantic and when her sister, Sooty, anounces her engagement the wedding becomes the most important thing in her life. Her own fantasies centre on Mick, the good-looking boy who works next door to her, and, when they meet and like each other, she longs for it to be 'forever and a day'. But real life has many unexpected twists of plot and when the dreamed-of moment comes, Marcy makes a surprising decision . . .

Follow that Dream 85p

Her parents' dream of moving to Cornwall is a nightmare blow for Sally. How could she bear to leave London and be stuck away in the country . . . with no mates, no music, no decent clothes, no parties and no Ben, just when she was getting somewhere with him? But the long-awaited visit from her best friend, Joanne, brings some unexpected conflicts and Sally finds her determination to remain apart slowly undermined by the presence of a boy called Danny . . .

Love, Emma 85p

Emma begins her nursing training with high hopes. Determined to achieve something for herself, she still finds the three-year separation from her established world of family and friends a little frightening. In letters to her parents, best friend and boyfriend – and in entries in her secret diary – Emma describes her new world in warm and witty detail . . . hard-working, occasionally exciting and always exhausting – but there are rewards; *and* a student doctor named Luke . . .

Anita Eires
Working Girl £1. 25

Jane Lovejoy's first day in her first job is a milestone in her life. Working for a large advertising agency is glamorous – even if she *was* only in the accounts department! Then, after joining the agency's social club, Jane rediscovers another attraction, Greg – the gorgeous guy she bumped into on the never-to-be-forgotten day of her final interview. Rumour has it that Greg puts work before pleasure, but when Jane sees him with the most attractive girl in the office, she knows his life isn't *all* work and no play . . .

Summer Awakening 85p

It was to be the holiday of a lifetime – two weeks in a villa in sunny Majorca. The whole family expected fun, sun and adventure, but when Lainie packed her daring new pink bikini she didn't expect the excitement of a boy as handsome and wealthy as Jonty. Could a holiday romance last? Lainie wasn't going to think about it – why worry about tomorrow when there is love in the sun and the sea?

Anthea Cohen
Dangerous Love 85p

Sandra isn't a dare-devil like her friend Edie, but she longs for the excitement of being with a wild crowd like Dan and his friends. During their quiet 'Sandra nights' she comes to know a different, more sensitive, Dan – yet there are still 'Dan nights' when he wants her to join in the excitement of the crowd and their dangerous schemes . . .

Danny's Girl 85p

For sixteen-year-old Wendy, life was pretty straightforward. She enjoyed her tomboy existence with her parents and brother Mike on their farm in Norfolk. Then, late one sunny September afternoon, Danny wandered into her life and suddenly Wendy's happy and uncomplicated world is turned upside-down. Unsure of how she should behave or what is expected of her, she allows herself to be carried along in Danny's wake, and when he finds himself in trouble at his exclusive boarding school she is his only ally. Eventually, Wendy's fierce loyalty to the boy she loves leads them both deeper and deeper into trouble . . .